Berlinguer and the Professor

Anonymous

Berlinguer and the Professor

Chronicles of the Next Italy

A Richard Seaver Book

The Viking Press · New York

Originally published in Italian as *Berlinguer e il Professore*
© 1975 by Rizzoli Editore Milan
English language translation Copyright © 1976 by The Viking Press, Inc.
A Richard Seaver Book/The Viking Press
First published in 1976 by The Viking Press, Inc.
625 Madison Avenue, New York 10022
Published simultaneously in Canada by
The Macmillan Company of Canada Limited
Printed in U.S.A.

Library of Congress Cataloging in Publication Data

Main entry under title:
Berlinguer and the professor.

"A Richard Seaver book."
Translation of Berlinguer e il professore.
PZ4.B5195   1975   [PQ4860.A1]   853′.9′14
ISBN 0-670-15882-8   75-35967

Note

Like all Italians, I too have often wondered how things are going to end. Thinking it over time and again, I realized that I was not succeeding by political analysis in finding any logical solution to the crisis in which we are foundering, and that the least irrational way of satisfying my curiosity was to let my imagination take over.

That is why I have adopted the guise of a secretary of Fanfani who in the year 2000 decides to tell all. And only under the protection afforded by anonymity have I been able to give free rein to the sincerity of my imagination.

Contents

Part One

I sit down to write this chronicle on returning from a ceremony that has filled me with pride. The author of these notes has had the privilege of riding with the minister of planning on the first nuclear-propulsion train, leaving the Campidoglio and arriving in the center of Palestrina in twenty-one-and-a-half minutes. As I mingled with the small crowd of officials who had the honor of accompanying the minister on this rapid yet comfortable journey from Rome's historical center to its outskirts, I will not conceal the fact that my eyelashes were bathed by a tear.

For someone like myself, who has spent all his life in the service of the Party and the nation, it would have been impossible to view with indifference the achievement of a sixteenth subway line, which, together with eleven elevated highways and twelve helicopter pads, has finally brought fluidity to the traffic of our metropolis. This imposing communications network, regulated by only nine traffic policemen assigned to three superelectronic brains, has made our capital one of the most progressive and socially advanced cities of the Fourth World.

A second tear coursed down my cheek as I listened to the dry, sober report delivered by the minister at the end of the trip. The Seven-Year Plan, known as the Great Restructuring, has transformed the face of the capital and of the entire peninsula. The millions of tourists who come every summer to visit the Italy of the year 2000 are no longer attracted by the monuments of the past—though these are by now perfectly restored and preserved—or even by our beaches, where the hotels in any case are only at the disposal of our workers for well-deserved vacations. They come to admire our highways, our school and hospital facilities, our farms, and the advanced techniques that have allowed our industrial plants to attain the highest volume of production at the lowest rate of pollution. Milan and Rome are the cities welcoming the greatest number of visitors. But whereas foreigners in Milan see the largest European financial center—the natural shelter for all American, German, and Swiss capital drawn by the stability of our currency—Rome plays host to experts in other fields. As the minister was able to note, there are few capitals boasting a more advanced urban-development plan. If one excepts Teheran, Kuwait, Abu Dhabi, and Cairo, there is no other city in the world that has made such progress. And to think that scarcely eight years ago, at the end of the Great Leap Forward but before the start of the Great Restructuring, the outskirts of Rome were still compared to the slums of Stockholm.

The idea of drafting these notes actually came to me during the trip from Rome to Palestrina and back. All of a sudden, I was reminded of another trip, one equally historical but much less rapid and by no means comfortable, that took place on January 20, way back in 1980. This journey, which few know about and of which even those few do not like to speak, had as its chief participants only two persons: a man still famous and honored today, I mean Amintore Fanfani, founder of the Second Italian Republic; and your humble servant, his zealous and devoted secretary.

We were both in Piazza del Gesù, then the headquarters of the Party, when final arrangements were made to go to the Farnesina Palace, a building demolished a few weeks after the proclamation of the Second Republic, along with all the other monuments left by the Fascist regime. This palace, not to be confused with the Farnesina in Via della Lungara that Agostino Chigi built for himself in 1510 and which later passed to the Farnese family, was a massive and dismal structure in white marble, and its demolition went unmourned by everyone. But in those years this marble shed was highly important, not only for the size of its halls and because it was the seat of the foreign ministry, but also for its fortunate location, far from the center of the city.

It was for this last reason that the shed had been picked as the ideal meeting place where the president of the Republic, Giovanni Leone, Prime Minister Ruggero Bertolon, and a number of ministers whose names today escape me were to receive Henry Kissinger, then merely the American secretary of state and scarcely at the beginning of that fabulous career that was to make him the central figure of world politics throughout the 1980s, until his sudden and disastrous fall, of which we all know. Fanfani, the most influential man in the Party, and whom I respectfully called the Professor, had also been invited.

The Farnesina shed had been picked on the heels of a secret-service report—by the SIDD (Information Service for Democratic Defense), to be exact—for in those tumultuous years it was not easy for anyone having the responsibility for public order to guarantee the safety of Italian and foreign political figures who were obliged to move from one part of the capital to another. Kissinger, for example, on his previous visit to Rome, had truly found himself in an awkward situation. A howling mob had assailed his bulletproof limousine, and the secretary of state was allowed to proceed only after the car had been covered with insulting inscriptions written in spray paint. American reporters wrote that they had never before witnessed such a scene and that no representative of the United States government had ever been greeted by so much animosity in a foreign country. The older ones recalled the uproar that had broken out in 1958 when Nixon had ridden through the streets of Caracas. But that had been nothing by comparison.

This bitter experience had led the SIDD to draw up a precise plan. The secretary of state's personal safety could be guaranteed only under these conditions: arrival of a United States aircraft carrier offshore from Fiumicino; Kissinger and his party to board five United States helicopters; the helicopters to land on the field of the Olympic Stadium; formation of a cortege of marines and Italian paratroopers to escort the secretary of state to the Farnesina, which lay no more than five hundred meters from the playing field.

The second problem, how to get Leone to the meeting, presented no difficulties. In fact, it was now some months since the president of the Republic had abandoned the Quirinale and moved to Villa Madama, following a lively episode that at first had created a sensation but in January 1980 was to turn out to be providential. It may be helpful to recall it, so that the reader will have a better understanding of the climate of those years, which though certainly turbulent were sometimes agreeably carefree.

By the middle of the 1970s, the Quirinale Palace had several times become the target for certain ill-intentioned persons. The newspapers of the time, with rightful indignation, had reported the text of a number of secret-service reports showing that, on at least four occasions, commandos of the far Right had planned to invade the palace and kidnap the head of state in order to compel him to annul the Constitution and promulgate a new one that would abolish the parliamentary republic and proclaim a presidential republic.

Nothing was ever known precisely about these attempted coups, but the threat, which was confirmed by official documents, had persuaded representatives of the more progressive political forces to take adequate security measures. And for some months groups of young people, sometimes supplied with chains and iron bars, sometimes with electric guitars, had bivouacked permanently in the large piazza in front of the palace. They spent the entire day singing revolutionary songs or improvising pop concerts. At night they got into their sleeping bags, posting a few sentries around a large fire left burning under the obelisk.

No one dared disturb them. And anyway these youngsters, who called themselves the Vigilantes, were performing a dual task that at the time seemed highly useful: they were safeguarding the president from the ulterior designs of the rightists, and they were reminding the president himself of the mood and sentiments of the more progressive part of the

Italian population. But one fine day the 185 members of the special *carabiniere* squad assigned to guard the president of the Republic, commonly known as cuirassiers, had announced a wildcat strike. On perceiving that the guards had let their rifles fall to the ground and had hastily abandoned their sentry boxes, the young people immediately ceased playing and singing. In their excitement or alarm, two thousand Vigilantes swarmed inside the palace, without encountering any resistance.

Faced with this invasion, the president at first thought he was going to have to live through the same dramatic hours once experienced by Louis XVI, when hordes of sans-culottes had arrived from Paris to penetrate the royal palace at Versailles. But history seldom repeats itself. Instead of bursting into the presidential apartments, the Vigilantes pushed toward the Coffee House, as the masonry pavilion rising in the center of the famous gardens of the Quirinale is still called. The Vigilantes began to set up tents and lay out sleeping bags under the trees and along the boxwood hedges. Once the strike was over, the cuirassiers resumed service, but took care not to interfere.

Cohabitation between the president and the Vigilantes nevertheless turned out to be difficult. The Quirinale kitchens found it very hard to see to the upkeep of an extra two thousand persons who demanded, not without logic, the same rations as the cuirassiers, since their purpose in being there was not to have a good time but to protect the president from right-wing plots. Furthermore it seems that Leone's consort, Donna Vittoria, found it unbecoming to her prestige and decorum as First Lady of the Republic that, in the gardens of her residence, male and female Vigilantes, and sometimes

Vigilantes of the same sex, paired off freely before the eyes of the cuirassiers.

But it was the president himself who was the most irritated. A tolerant and sociable man, he might have been able to adapt himself even to this invasion, in any case a peaceful one. But what was unbearable to him were the sounds of the electric guitars emanating from the Coffee House, transmitted full blast far into the night by loudspeakers set up in the garden. This music was especially disagreeable to someone like himself, who was a great connoisseur and even a fairly good performer of Neapolitan songs.

The president set out to devise a plan of escape. He personally consulted the historical texts, not only to find out how Louis XVI had behaved when he had abandoned the palace of the Tuileries, where he was being held hostage by the sans-culottes, but also so as not to repeat the tragic mistakes that had delivered the French sovereign into the hands of the postilion Drouet, the man who had arrested him at Varennes.

Louis XVI had had to leave by night, since the Tuileries were guarded like a prison. A guard was stationed at every exit; six hundred armed militiamen garrisoned the gardens, the courtyard, and the large terrace. In the antechambers and salons, valets and Swiss guards won over to the revolutionary cause slept across the doorways. Louis XVI and Marie Antoinette were therefore obliged to flee at midnight. Leone, on the other hand, with far less difficulties to face, could even have left at noon. The youngsters stationed in the gardens kept very little watch on those who came in; they kept no watch at all on those who went out.

Louis XVI and Marie Antoinette had abandoned the Tuileries disguised as servants. But Donna Vittoria and Giovanni Leone rejected any such suggestion with steadfastness and dignity. Nor did the president have any difficulty in understanding that the sovereign's escape plan, while carefully prepared, had a single but obvious weak point: the length of the journey from Paris to Metz, where General Bouillé's army was awaiting him. The longer the journey, argued the president with his well-known sagacity, the greater the probability of ugly surprises. And he therefore refused the fond assurances of Domenico and Davide Pellegrini, administrators respectively of the hunting estates of Castelporziano and San Rossore, that they would be happy to offer him the most secure of refuges. The goal of the journey would instead be Villa Madama, located on the slopes of Monte Mario and only seven kilometers from the Quirinale.

Louis XVI, however, had had one point in his favor. Once he had eluded the surveillance of the gendarmes and spies who filled the palace, the sovereign's flight had been easy, thanks to a carriage drawn by four post-horses. The flight of the Leone family promised to be much more difficult. A limousine was out of the question. Ever since the price of gasoline had risen to a thousand liras a liter* and the Romans had had to go about on bicycles, exasperated crowds had flung themselves shouting at any official automobile that appeared on the horizon. Neither the president nor still less Donna Vittoria would have thought it dignified to leave the Quirinale by taxi, on foot, or even by bicycle. Anyway these means of locomotion were also to be avoided for another reason: Leone and consort would have been immediately recognized. Their faces had appeared too many times on television screens.

* About $6.67 a gallon. (Translator.)

Louis XVI's carriage was much envied, until Nino Valentino, private secretary and press attaché to the president, came up with the right idea. He in fact was the one to suggest what has gone down in history as "Operation Gianco."

Giancarlo Leone (Gianco to his friends), one of the president's sons, did not stay at the Quirinale with his father, but instead lived alone, on his own means, being the head of Leonfoto, a thriving photographic studio specializing in the reproduction of pictures of the head of state and of Donna Vittoria for use in ministries, public offices, and schools. Gianco owned a Volkswagen station wagon, which on this occasion turned out to be providential. Indeed it was easy for Gianco to enter the Quirinale with his station wagon, load his father, mother, and brothers into it, leave undisturbed, and rapidly drive to Villa Madama.

The flight of Leone—if it is legitimate to speak of an actual flight—had produced a sensation in political circles, but was received almost with indifference by public opinion. The newspapers, however, reported it as a temporary move. Not even the Vigilantes gave this incident undue importance, and they judged it inconvenient to transfer themselves to the slopes of Monte Mario. They stayed in the Quirinale, and the cuirassiers, instead of throwing them out, ended by fraternizing with them.

On the large square in front of the Coffee House, reached from the park by a short flight of steps, a bandstand was built, and the best pop and folksong groups of the capital took turns in appearing. A permanent Festival of the Democratic Republic was organized. The radical leader Marco Pannella was unanimously proclaimed administrator of the Quirinale, in the absence of the rightful tenant.

The Vigilantes were content, the president more than content. Leone loved Villa Madama, less magnificent, but quiet and surrounded by greenery. And from there the president could easily reach, even on foot, the only two places that by now he ever had occasion to visit: the Farnesina, where the increasingly infrequent receptions for foreign personalities were held, and the adjoining Olympic Stadium, where every Sunday he and his family attended the soccer match.

"Let them manage by themselves." With these words the SIDD report shrugged off the problem of protecting Ruggero Bertolon and those other ministers whose names for the moment escape me. But this seeming arrogance of the secret service can be explained. In the first place, this Ruggero Bertolon, having been named prime minister barely six weeks before, and having taken care never to be photographed or to appear on television, was virtually unknown to all Italians except his friends, and these lived in Marostica, in the province of Vicenza. All Bertolon had to do was to give up his official car and get to the Farnesina by his own means, in a taxi as far as possible, then on foot, mingling with the passersby so as to be even more inconspicuous. Besides, it should be remembered that Bertolon and his twenty ministers were considered in the Italy of that time as figures of no importance whatsoever.

The reason will be explained in due course. For the moment, suffice it to note that though their presence was indeed thought indispensable for official ceremonies, it never occurred to anyone to sacrifice a single traffic policeman for the protection of their safety. Public opinion, in fact, demonstrated an almost total indifference to the kidnapping, sequestration, and even murder of politicians, especially those who formed part of the government. To give an example: just a week before, the corpse of an undersecretary had been recovered at the bottom of a steep slope, the skull crushed by an iron bar. The news had been reported very briefly on the inside pages of all the daily papers.

On the other hand, the SIDD report devoted the most meticulous attention to the transporting of the Professor. The reasons for this preferential treatment were rather complex and should be explained to a contemporary reader both carefully and frankly. This is what I intend to do, and the sincere, almost filial, affection that I felt for this man over a long period of my life will certainly not hinder me in my duty as a chronicler to tell the truth. And the truth, unfortunately, is this: in that remote January 1980 the Professor was simultaneously the most important man in Italy and the man most disliked by the Italians.

According to the latest public opinion poll, which he himself had ordered, the execration index when it came to him had risen to eighty-two per cent, as against thirteen per cent for those who hated him and five per cent for those who merely loathed him. There were many reasons for this widespread unpopularity. The parties and movements on the Left considered the Professor the symbol of the arrogance of power. His Christian Democrat friends by now found him an irritating and conceited old man. But the former did not judge it convenient to overthrow him, convinced as they were that without him it would be hard to find another single objective at which to direct popular rage. The latter, all of whom would have liked to oust him, were unable to agree on who should take his place.

For months the Professor, increasingly detested but increasingly untouchable, had not left Piazza del Gesù, officially the Party headquarters, but which over the years had become his personal residence. Perhaps through an abrupt change of mood or perhaps so as not to succumb to the inertia that had been forced on him, the Professor had given up painting, something for which he had long been rightly famous, and had turned to sculpture. To allow him to pursue his new activity in the best way possible, the top floor of the building had been transformed into a studio. In a spacious hall, created by knocking out all the dividing walls, a single huge block of marble had been installed, and the Professor busied himself around it from dawn to dusk.

The chisel was held firmly by a still steady hand. In his other hand he brandished a mallet, planting on the chisel the most energetic blows, like those stoneworkers who used to chip flint at the beginning of the twentieth century.

To no one, not even to me, had the Professor revealed what the subject was to be of the work on which he had set out with such grim intensity, and nothing could be glimpsed since it would take him at least a year of hard labor to shape that giant block. I can only say that the difficulty of the undertaking and its almost superhuman toil exalted him. In his moments of greatest dedication, when sparks flew from the chisel as it struck the marble, I had sometimes found him singing.

The marble seemed to have obsessed him to the point of forgetting the affairs of the Party (about which in any case he did not bother to keep up-to-date). The dining room, on the second floor of the palace, remained generally deserted. The sculptor had a frugal repast brought to the studio by an old peasant woman, whom he had chosen as his housekeeper and cook. Only I had the privilege, and that not always, of keeping him company.

The old woman would come up at noon on the dot, carrying the food enveloped in a large cloth, in the manner of Tuscan farm workers. The Professor would lay aside his chisel and mallet, descend from the scaffold set up beside the monolith, untie the cloth, and at the sight of the food let out a few small cries of satisfaction. The old woman prepared simple, healthy dishes: bread and tomato purée, beans with olive oil, beef stew with potatoes, cabbage soup. Punctually every Sunday chicken *alla cacciatora* made its appearance.

The Professor ate heartily, one might even say voraciously, watering the purée with a thin wine from Pieve Santo Stefano. As soon as he had gulped down the last mouthful, without even allowing himself to pause for coffee or a cigarette, the Professor returned to his mallet and chisel. Often he forgot to wipe a napkin across his mouth and beard, that flowing white beard which he had been letting grow for the past year. So great was his ardor for his chisel that he ignored the few bean skins and bits of cabbage that still clung to the hairs around his mouth.

It was not easy to persuade the Professor to separate himself from his faithful chisel when I myself announced to him the arrival of General Maletti, head of the SIDD, who had come to explain to him the detailed plan for transporting him from Piazza del Gesù to the Farnesina. While the general was laying out and reading the little maps that established the salient moments of the operation, it seemed as though the Professor were only half listening. But I knew him too well to be fooled. Actually I had immediately understood that the Professor was very interested, not only in Kissinger's visit but in the Maletti Plan as well.

Otherwise he would have behaved quite differently. The Professor could easily have made the general wait for two hours in the vestibule, deafening him with constant blows of the hammer, or even with the fearful sound of an electric saw, which he sometimes used to cut small slabs of marble. After this sort of treatment, the two deputies Forlani and Malfatti, the last to appear in Piazza del Gesù, had never been seen again. Or the Professor might have received the general immediately, embracing him effusively and inviting him, before he had a chance to open his mouth, to lend a hand with the chisel and mallet. The general would not have known how to get out of it, nor would he have been able to keep up with the rhythm that the Professor imparted to his own blows. After a quarter of an hour, the general would have left the mallet on the scaffold and rapidly taken his leave. The only man to withstand at any length this test of strength, of ability, and in a certain sense of faith had been Senator Bartolomei. But he, after twenty-five minutes, either from fatigue or because the rhythm was becoming more and more insistent, instead of hitting the head of the chisel, had mashed two fingers of his left hand with the mallet.

General Maletti, unaware of the dangers he had been spared, was able to explain his plan with complete tranquillity. To transport the Professor, he had not prepared complicated security measures and had limited himself to certain expedients that to today's reader will seem extravagant, but which in the climate of those years were serious and elementary.

Given the habit of Roman cyclists to hurl themselves at every automobile that appeared on the horizon, it was not suitable to use an official car. If then the cyclists were to realize that it was the Professor who was traveling in the car, the secret service would no longer be accountable for whatever might happen. Not even a lynching was out of the question. A more suitable idea was to send to the garage for that armored vehicle in which Kissinger, as you know, had had such a bad experience. The body of the limousine was still dented all over from the stones of the demonstrators, and this had been the main reason why Kissinger had got rid of it, leaving it to the Italian government in exchange for an Etruscan vase. But the armored doors were still bulletproof. The insulting inscriptions, which had been written with spray paint, had disappeared once the garage attendant had given the car a coat of glazed enamel. The engine had done more than sixty thousand miles but still appeared to be in good condition.

The limousine, which Romans good-naturedly called the Wreck, offered one great advantage: it was furnished with a powerful radio transmitter and receiver that had allowed Kissinger, no matter what part of the world he was in, to keep in constant contact with the White House. And the general had stationed some fifty agents, each equipped with a radio, along all the possible itineraries from Piazza del Gesù to the Farnesina, to signal to the Professor's driver the streets least clogged by cyclists. In this way, by proceeding at a sustained speed, the car would at least be able to come within proximity of the Olympic Stadium.

But to go from Piazza del Gesù to the Farnesina, one necessarily had to cross the Tiber, and at this point, for the general and thus for the Professor as well, a serious obstacle had arisen. It was in those years, in fact, that a new form of protest had become widespread. The more advanced political and trade-union forces had taken control of all the Tiber bridges for the purpose of financing those categories of workers who at the moment were engaged in struggle.

Roadblocks had been set up at the entrances to all the bridges: scooter drivers, cyclists, and pedestrians passed in single file through a narrow opening, after paying the toll to the custodian. Bus riders had to get off, cross the bridge on foot, and wait for a second bus on the other side of the river. Should a rare official car arrive, or an even rarer private car, the custodians, before removing the block and giving the go-ahead signal, naturally demanded an adequate toll.

To try to force these blocks was foolhardy, and it was madness to arrive with the Wreck. The custodians would insist on an inspection, and once they discovered who had sought asylum behind those armored doors, they would certainly not let him get away. Nor could the general promise to come to his aid. Aside from the doubtful loyalty of the police, and in this particular case of the armed forces themselves, the general had no intention of assuming the responsibility for a show of force that might even lead to civil war. Blocked at a bridge, the Professor would have to look out for himself. The very least that could happen to him would be the disbursement of an exorbitant toll.

Maletti had nevertheless singled out an opening in the enemy ranks. In the still picturesque Rome of those years, a little beyond the Flaminio Bridge and thus not too far from the Farnesina, a pontoon bridge was still in operation, a Bailey bridge constructed by the Allies during the Second World War and that no one had since thought to demolish. But it had fallen into disuse, since cyclists and scooter drivers did not care to take on its disjointed roadbed. The checkpoint set up by the custodians at this bridge was actually quite fragile. They themselves, to overcome their boredom, spent the whole day on the other side of the street watching the children play soccer.

The Wreck, proceeding at a steady speed along the Tiber and arriving at the Bailey bridge, would then have to make a sharp left turn. To force the checkpoint, almost surely unguarded, would be easy. From then on, neither the armored car nor its precious passenger would run any risk. Waiting for them on the other side of the river would be stationed a solid detachment of Gurkhas.

How was it that these Nepali warriors, once the pride of the British army and the terror of the Indian masses, found themselves in the vicinity of the Milvio Bridge in that January of 1980? The reader deserves an explanation, even at the cost of delaying the outcome of the Maletti Plan.

To understand what had happened, we must actually go way back to the end of 1975, when the newspapers began to report kidnappings by certain anonymous groups that were much more efficient and better equipped than the gangs of Mafiosi and brotherhoods of Sardinian bandits who until then had had the monopoly of such activities. The facility with which the rich disbursed ransom money, the inefficiency of the police, the sagacity of the kidnappers, who preferred to reinvest their initial profits rather than squander them or send them to Switzerland, all helped to make these anonymous exploits something to be respected. Already by the end of 1976 people had begun to speak of *nouveaux riches* who were boldly setting out to scale the heights of the industrial and financial world.

In the face of this concrete threat, the old rich closed ranks. After some stormy meetings at the offices of the Confindustria,* after long negotiations with the government, after very long—and very secret—negotiations with the opposition and the trade unions, it was finally possible to launch an

* Italian Manufacturers' Association. (Tr.)

emergency program. The minister of foreign trade authorized the importation of Gurkhas by any Italian citizen, provided he had a clean record and was disposed to sign them up for a five-year contract to be paid in advance in gold, silver, or hard currency, to be deposited in a bank in Katmandu. The minister of the interior allowed every imported Gurkha, on his arrival at Fiumicino airport, to be issued a permit to carry firearms.

The enterprise had happy results, and already by the beginning of 1977 there was a radical change in the situation. Gurkhas, officially employed as butlers, footmen, and chauffeurs, performed the excellent work that one had every reason to expect from such efficient, loyal, and, when occasion demanded, fierce soldiers. In a few months the profits of the anonymous kidnappers had become negligible. But instead of ceasing, the importations continued. Though their children could then go back to attending even the public schools with complete tranquillity, tycoons and bankers went on adding to their Gurkha staffs in a frankly excessive manner. No magnate dared to show up for a reception or business conference without leaving a retinue of armed men outside the door. The platoon of Gurkhas had taken the place of the private airplane and the yacht as the status symbol of the ruling class.

Middle and small manufacturers, successful surgeons and prominent lawyers, directors, actors, and stockbrokers did not wish to lag behind the oil and automobile magnates. Soon all the society ladies of Milan insisted on being accompanied to the dressmaker or the milliner by two or three mustachioed brutes. The ladies did not want their escorts to wear their usual dreary uniforms and ransacked the storerooms of opera houses to rent boots that rose halfway up the thigh, plumed hats, bandoliers, sashes, peaked hats. Even rare pistols, with mother-of-pearl butts, appeared on the wide belts of the Gurkhas.

But the decriers of customs, of whom there was no lack even in those carefree and dissolute times, for once had the satisfaction of seeing their dark prophecies come true. Thanks to a recession that suddenly struck the already fragile economy, the Gurkha craze ceased almost at one stroke.

This is what happened: Because of some administrative hitch, the American government postponed a loan to Italy by a few weeks. A cold wave of austerity fell on the more humble classes; street demonstrations became more frequent and threatening; and the rich, seized by panic, sought refuge in Switzerland. All Italians, in short, were plunged into crisis. All except one: Eugenio Cefis, then only the president of Montedison.* It was during those dramatic months that Cefis was able to lay the foundations for his fabulous personal fortune, which transformed him into the czar of the economy until he was overtaken by his final and clamorous fall.

* A state-controlled chemical complex. (Tr.)

And yet Eugenio Cefis, respectfully known as the Doctor, had at first seemed to be the entrepreneur in the greatest difficulty. As soon as the storm broke, his business rival, backed by obscure financiers, had in fact begun to buy up all the available Montedison shares on the market. It was not the first time that someone had tried to take over that petrochemical conglomerate, but on this occasion the Doctor did not show the same grim face and readiness to act that he had often displayed under similar circumstances in the past. Yet his controlling interest in the company seemed seriously threatened.

But it was not only the Montedison affair that was troubling the Milanese financial operators. The Gurkha affair seemed more alarming still. As already noted, the Gurkhas had been imported upon payment in advance; now it should be added that, in exchange for this outlay, the importer obtained the right to use his Gurkhas however he saw fit. He could even resell them, up to the expiration of the contract, but only within the confines of Italy.

Since the beginning of 1976, a small Gurkha market had been set up in Milan, frequented chiefly by ladies of limited financial means in search of a good bargain. But now the exodus to Switzerland by all of Milanese society had flooded this little market with thousands of contracts. Everyone was selling off those mustachioed and unexportable brutes. A Gurkha worth thirty or forty million liras scarcely six months before on the public square of Katmandu was offered for two million on the streets of Milan.

While Montedison shares continued to rise, Gurkha contracts continued to sink. One man alone realized the fabulous opportunity afforded him by this chance coincidence. By the time rivals realized it, it was too late. The Doctor had already invested in Gurkha contracts the money he had obtained by relinquishing his Montedison shares to the operators.

"**N**ow just let anyone try to screw around with me." With these coarse words, the Doctor greeted his financial expert, the faithful Corsi, who was waving Gurkha Contract No. 12,772, just acquired at the market for 750,000 liras. "That's enough for the moment," added the Doctor. "Now all we have to do is go on the offensive. The hour has sounded for the counterattack." Ever since the time when he was a cadet at the military academy in Modena, and since his heroic days in the Partisan struggle, the Doctor had always liked to express himself in military terms, and he had preserved the brusque and hurried manners of a soldier. That same evening, escorted by twelve thousand Gurkhas, the Doctor paid a visit to the rival who had summoned him to clarify the controversial question of the controlling shares. After barely twenty-three minutes of discussion, it was the rival himself who advanced the proposal, benignly accepted, to resell to the Doctor, at their nominal value, all the Montedison shares that he had just bought up.

Next day, while the newspapers were reporting the sensational transaction on the front page and describing the picturesque cortege of Gurkhas through the center of Milan, the Doctor was in Rome, in the office of Ferdinando Ventriglia, who had finally succeeded Guido Carli as governor of the Banca d'Italia. Without wasting time on preliminaries, the Doctor immediately came to the point: "My dear Ventriglia, since I'm stopping off in Rome, I've come to say hello and let you know a decision I've made. Beginning next month, I intend to start minting coins." Noting a slight expression of stupor on Ventriglia's face, the Doctor hastened to reassure him. "I said mint coins, not print bills of ten or a hundred thousand liras, which between you and me I wouldn't know how to do anyway. I'm going to mint gold napoleons and silver scudi, with the image of Enrico Mattei on one side and 'Montedison' inscribed on the other. These coins will be legal tender all over Italy. And don't tell me it's not possible. With the political friends you have, you can get me any license I need." Before the governor could reply, the Doctor had already left.

Next morning, back in his Foro Bonaparte office in Milan, the Doctor received the trade-union representatives for all his firms. Gurkhas garrisoned the premises. "Firm understandings make firm friends," he began. "Beginning next month, I will be in a position to offer you your remuneration in gold and silver coins, safe from any inflationary rise or speculative maneuver. All I ask in exchange is your pledge not to press any wage or work-rule demands for the next five years. Take it or leave it. But let it be clear: anyone who leaves it also leaves Montedison. My helpers will see to it that any eventual departures take place in an orderly fashion."

The next day the Doctor decided to remedy the only foolish operation in which he had ever indulged in all his years of business activity. At the beginning of the 1970s, he had been inexplicably attacked by the disease of printed paper and had acquired some of the more important national dailies. It had brought him nothing but trouble: unruly reporters, ineffectual or incapable editors, complaints from politicians, enormous deficits. Now the Doctor had before him a small crowd of delegated advisers, editors, and reporters' committees. This time there was not even the semblance of a preamble. "As of midnight tonight," said the Doctor, "I have decided to give up the publication of all the newspapers under my control. Now no one can go on claiming that I use the press for political purposes. All of you, and all the reporters you represent, will nevertheless have the choice of remaining in the firms of the Montedison complex. I can offer you the compilation of advertising folders. But as piecework."

Everyone looked to the most important representative of the newspapermen's union. In his turn, the representative looked with dismay at the faces of the Gurkhas guarding the entrance. He steeled himself, however. "Perhaps we could . . ." he began. "No." The Doctor cut him short.

In three days Cefis had laid the foundations for what was to be the most fabulous business success of the century. He could now count on a long trade-union peace in a country convulsed by strikes, and he had freed himself, as he liked to express it, from the last dry branches, that is to say from those damned newspapers that in 1975 alone had consumed tens of billions of liras and brought him endless trouble.

The Doctor had won, but it was not his intention to overdo it. He himself was the first to realize that he could not long keep twelve thousand Gurkhas parading through the streets of Milan. If his enemies, defeated but uncrushed, should begin to attribute to him the intention of carrying out a coup d'état, his position would become difficult. Those mustachioed brutes, so useful insofar as they multiplied his powers of persuasion in the negotiations phase, became dangerously cumbersome once an accord was reached.

A close student of military matters, the Doctor had assimilated the lesson of Grechko, the Soviet marshal who, having accomplished the occupation of Czechoslovakia by a handbook operation, had also been able to grasp all the delicacy and importance of certain logistic problems that are usually neglected. "Every Czech and every Slovak," the marshal had said, "must know that my men remain on their territory, but no one should be able to see them."

That Sunday the Doctor was in Rome, to confer with a high prelate of the Curia. Cefis offered His Eminence, at the token price of one thousand liras, the entire block of controlling shares in the Società Generale Immobiliare,* of which the Vatican had been the fond first owner. In exchange, he obtained for five years the legal right to use twelve monasteries, sixty-three convents, and sixteen seminaries, scattered here and there all over the peninsula, and uninhabited because of the decline in vocations. Here all the Gurkhas were decently and discreetly lodged. So as not to make a needless show of strength, the Doctor had even given up his bodyguard.

* General Real Estate Company. (Tr.)

As chance, or perhaps Providence, would have it, one of the seminaries assigned to the Gurkhas was located on the slopes of Monte Mario. General Maletti had personally gone to Milan to implore the Doctor to lend him these men for a mission that would take up only a single afternoon and that in any case was of great importance for national security. The Doctor had hedged, it being his firm principle not to lend Gurkhas, but when he had learned that the very safety of the Professor was at stake, he was unable to say no.

And so General Maletti was able to announce, with legitimate pride, that two hundred Gurkhas, dressed as priests and seminarians, would be on hand to welcome the armored car on the other side of the Bailey bridge.

"Excellent!" exclaimed the Professor. "It looks to me like a perfect plan." The general went away confused, stammering a few words of thanks.

No sooner had Maletti left than the Professor seemed another man. Though it was barely three in the afternoon, he abruptly put an end to his daily toil, arranging chisels and mallets in good order along the scaffold. Then he ran to a corner of the studio and came back carrying a bundle of plastic sheets in his strong arms. I helped him spread them out and shake them to remove the dust that had collected on them. Then together we packaged the shapeless marble monolith, in the manner of the sculptor Christo.

The Maletti Plan did in fact turn out to be perfect. For the first time in Italian history something ordered by a military man had been carried out to the letter. The armored doors of the car withstood a volley of stones organized, or rather improvised, in Corso Vittorio. The Tiber embankment was covered at a steady speed. On reaching the Bailey bridge, the driver executed a left turn that was simply perfect: all that was left was to dislodge, with the front bumper of the car, a tree trunk lying across the road to block traffic. The custodians were indeed on the other side of the street, admiring twenty-two small boys playing soccer. Taken by surprise, they confined themselves to waving their fists in the air and hurling a few imprecations that naturally the Professor did not catch, perhaps would not even have understood. On the other side of the bridge, those priests and seminarians who seemed to have found themselves there by chance during their afternoon walk had already formed a protective circle.

The armored limousine was able to enter the courtyard of the building only a minute and thirty seconds later than its anticipated arrival. The Professor had plenty of time to shake hands with President Leone, Prime Minister Bertolon, and the twenty ministers, all of whom were present. The chief of protocol invited him to take his place at the end of the line that had already formed to welcome the guest. Kissinger, likewise very punctual, arrived barely eight minutes later, preceded by forty Italian paratroopers and followed by an equal number of marines. Everyone noted that his step was a little too springy and his smile a little too carefree.

The ceremony was simple and brief. Kissinger said that in the face of "urgent and desperate" appeals by the Italian government, the United States administration had once again consented to extend a loan of four billion dollars. As security, the administration had accepted fifty-six paintings from the Uffizi Gallery. The four billion dollars would be deposited in the Banca d'Italia, but not before the Italian government had placed, under each of the fifty-six paintings, a small brass plate on which was to be inscribed: "United States Government Property." This plate could be removed only when the entire amount of the loan had been repaid.

Ruggero Bertolon, reading from a typewritten sheet drawn up in accord with the opposition parties and the trade unions, responded with dignity and pride. Omitting any reference to dollars or brass plates, the prime minister confined himself to thanking Kissinger for having said that he found an orderly, hardworking Italy, democratically and socially advanced, in short an Italy very different from the one usually described in the American press.

Actually Kissinger had said nothing of the kind, but none of the listeners, either on the Italian or the American side, gave any sign of noticing the all-too-obvious contradictions between the two official speeches. This behavior can be understood if one keeps in mind what the political and diplomatic relations between Italy and the United States were like in those years. These relations were indeed of an entirely special kind. To define them, the experts spoke of "parallel divergences."

In those years the government of the United States also had its troubles. On the economic front, the Americans could not complain, since after the discovery of huge oil deposits in Arkansas and the drastic reduction in military expenditures passed into law by Congress, the balance of payments closed each year with a comfortable margin of assets. But this new boom was accompanied by an equal decline in United States prestige and influence in the world. The Americans, made indolent by prosperity and still reeling from their unfortunate adventure in Vietnam, had come to consider all international obligations a nuisance. In a short time the mood of a nation once known as the policeman of the world had profoundly changed. No one, for instance, could have imagined at the beginning of the 1970s that the same Americans who had risked their lives in the jungles of Vietnam would, only eight years later, calmly watch on their television screens the entry of the first Arab paratroopers into Tel Aviv. No one would have thought that toward the end of the 1970s the political struggle would no longer be between Republicans and Democrats, but between hard-line isolationists, who demanded the immediate closing of all embassies and consulates abroad, and the more moderate isolationists, committed to progressive disengagement.

Kissinger, who was without doubt the most consistent architect of this latter theory, had accepted the dismemberment of Israel and Turkey's entrance into the Warsaw Pact, and had not reacted when a pro-Soviet marshal was installed in Yugoslavia in place of Tito, nor when, shortly after the death of Franco, a leftist military junta had taken power in

Spain. Nevertheless, he still considered premature any decision to let Italy slide into the area of Soviet influence.

The secretary of state thus thought it indispensable, at least for the time being, to keep the Italian political system on its feet and prevent an economic collapse, and he was ready to grant the government in Rome frequent and even generous loans. But it was not so easy to find a way to give Italy this money. To the hard-line isolationists, Kissinger had to demonstrate that these dollars were not being thrown to the wind and that, in any case, they were covered by strict guarantees. To the trade unions and opposition parties, Bertolon had to demonstrate that the Italian government was not prepared to accept anything which smacked of subsidies and foreign aid. In short, Kissinger and Bertolon were united by a common interest. The first was happy to disburse these dollars; the other was happy to receive them. But Kissinger was ready to disburse them on condition that people knew about it, whereas Bertolon was ready to receive them on condition that no one knew. Here, in brief, were the parallel divergences.

Negotiations were long and difficult and engaged the finest diplomatic minds in both countries; nevertheless, a compromise was reached that was acceptable to both sides. Every six months the Americans would grant a loan of four billion dollars, while receiving as security our works of art, but they bound themselves not to require their transfer to museums in Washington or New York. For its part, the Italian government bound itself to attach the small brass plates under the pictures, so as to reassure United States tourists about the quality of the investments made by their secretary of state.

But it was not easy for the Italian government to sell this compromise to the opposition parties and especially to sell it to the trade unions. There was the obvious objection that even in this way national dignity would be impaired, that intellectuals and men of culture would never accept such a shameful mortgage. Then who was to guarantee that the mortgage would be only a formality? And that it was not all a CIA plan to land the marines under the pretext of taking possession of the paintings?

The diplomatic minds had to go back to work. Agreement was reached only when the government pledged itself never to declare, officially, that it had received anything from the United States. In exchange, the trade unions and opposition parties promised not to raise indelicate questions either in the newspapers or in Parliament. There remained the disagreeable question of the brass plates, which Kissinger had absolutely no intention of giving up. The government promised the trade unions to inscribe "United States Government Property" in very small letters and to order the museum attendants never to polish them.

This difficult but important compromise had remained in force for over two years. That afternoon in January 1980 was now the fifth time that Kissinger had arrived in Rome with a check for four billion dollars. Hundreds of little brass plates had already been affixed in the Pinacoteca di Brera in Milan, the Museo Nazionale and Museo d'Arte Moderna in Rome, and the Uffizi in Florence. The minister of culture (who in all those years, except for a few brief interruptions, was Giovanni Spadolini) kept careful watch, sometimes in person, to make sure that no provocateur polished any of them at night.

Had President Leone been offering the dinner, protocol would have required at least five courses. Fifty liveried footmen in knee breeches, almost all of them retired cuirassiers, would have served at table and poured at least two kinds of wine, as well as champagne, not of that year but of quality. Had he been the host, Leone would have had to call on Cavalier Volpini, banquet chief, who would have seen to the table settings *de rigueur* in such circumstances: dishes of Sèvres porcelain, crystal once belonging to the Bourbons, gold-plated silverware, six-branched candelabra. On Cavalier Volpini's incontestable judgment depended whether fifty footmen would be sufficient or if it was necessary to summon reinforcements from the Black Capes—waiters recruited from the most famous pastry shops in the capital and provided for the occasion with a special livery.

But Cavalier Volpini had appeared reluctant. The Quirinale chefs, Cavaliers Pacifici and Nibbi, who had unwillingly adapted themselves to preparing food for the two thousand Vigilantes, had accepted with enthusiasm, but Cavalier Caligaris, superintendent of the Quirinale cellars, had replied that the Vigilantes had used up everything. The retired cuirassiers were seeking to follow the example of their younger colleagues and trying to fraternize with the Vigilantes. The potential Black Capes were on strike.

Had the foreign minister been offering the dinner, things would have been simpler, since protocol provided that the food, waiters, and even the table settings be furnished by the Grand

Hotel. But, unfortunately, the cooks and waiters of the Grand Hotel had stated that they would never submit to serving the American secretary of state.

The concrete possibility of leaving Kissinger supperless was avoided thanks to the sympathy of the trade-union representatives, who took pains to inform the chief protocol officer that they were ready for the fullest cooperation on condition that, in the name of the dignity of the Italian people and the name of world brotherhood, the dinner was prepared by the cooks of their organization's mess, with the help of UNA-COMAE, the cooperative set up by employees of the ministry. The mess would provide *pastasciutta* and an apple for each guest; UNACOMAE would supply chickens cooked on the electric rotisserie in its supermarket, as well as some local Roman table wine.

The only concession: a glass of *spumante* for each place. But the toasts were unusually concise. Bertolon got up, saying only, "To your health." Kissinger got up in his turn, raised his glass, and said nothing.

Once the dinner was over, Bertolon, the Professor, and the twenty attending ministers took leave of Kissinger, shaking his hand as soon as he got to the door. The only one offering to accompany the guest was the head of state.

Even this detail of the ceremony had been the fruit of long negotiations between the dean of diplomatic protocol and the trade unions. According to the dean, the representative of a foreign country, even if it were the United States, ought to be accompanied to the airport, or in this case the playing field of the Olympic Stadium, where the helicopters awaited him. According to the trade unionists, in a highly advanced democracy such as Italy certainly was, the workers didn't give a damn about protocol and all other musty diplomatic customs. Besides, the workers would lose whatever faith and residual esteem they had for the president of the Republic should Leone push his servility to the point of seeing the representative of the most odious capitalist state in the Western world off in his helicopter.

It was a young diplomat, the same one who had the idea of not polishing the brass plates on the paintings, who found a way out that allowed the government and trade unions to save face. At the moment when Kissinger was to leave the dining room, just before finding himself alone with his American entourage in the endless dreary corridors of the Farnesina, the president was to step forward and exclaim: "I'll come with you. Anyway, we're going the same way." Which in fact was true, since Leone, in order to return to his refuge in Villa Madama, had to pass the Olympic Stadium.

After some resistance, the trade unions ended by agreeing, on condition that the president say good-bye to Kissinger in front of the entrance to the stadium, without actually going onto the playing field where the helicopters stood ready.

And so Leone took Kissinger by the arm, the latter slightly surprised at this unexpected breeze of cordiality, and prodded him into the elevator. But at this point Ruggero Bertolon, the twenty ministers, and the Professor (who had charged me to remain at his side), instead of exchanging a few more remarks on the threshold and then each departing on his own, returned to the dining room and closed the door behind them. And this was a decision that had by no means been cleared with the trade unions. A decision, indeed, that the trade unions had in no way foreseen.

Part Two

The waiters hurriedly cleared away the knives and forks, the glasses, the plates with the apple peels. The long table where Kissinger had consumed the most frugal supper of his career had now become a work table. The Professor seated himself in the place of honor, with Bertolon as prime minister on his right, and the others took their places in no particular order. Having been asked to remain as secretary and take down the minutes of the meeting, I took a seat at the far end, away from everyone. I was facing the Professor, but in vain did I seek, by scrutinizing his gaze, to guess what he was up to.

After a few seconds, which seemed interminable, the Professor began to speak: "My dear and illustrious friends, first of all, I thank you for having accepted the invitations sent secretly to you, and for having made haste to appear at the ceremony we have just now concluded. But I would be doing an injustice to your acumen, and to your vigilant political awareness, were I to believe that you have come here merely to shake hands with an American. If you are now seated at this table, it is because you are expecting some important communication. My dear and illustrious friends, I will try not to disappoint you."

Knowing him well, I understood that perhaps the Professor did have something important to communicate, but he certainly seemed in no hurry to come to the point. And indeed he asked me to hand him a leather briefcase that he had entrusted to me before boarding the armored limousine in

Piazza del Gesù. He took out a large file—it must have contained at least 150 pages—put on his glasses, and began to read aloud in the toneless voice of a notary. It was a report on "The State of the Party from May 12, 1974, to January 12, 1980."

Not even this time did the Professor have any intention of giving up his usual tactics, which consisted in lulling the tension of his listeners, even at the cost of boring them, and engaging in a test of resistance with his more hostile opponents. His reports were written in a crabbed style, his arguments put forth in a painful, contorted, and sometimes cryptic form. But it was his most inaccessible sentences that turned out, in the long run, to be the most functional. In his many years of political life, the Professor had perfected a sure instinct: just when his audience seemed exhausted, he would unveil a motion, an order of the day, or a communiqué, which would then be unanimously approved.

But, so as not to tax unduly the reader's patience, I will outline the gist of those 150 pages, integrating it all with an account of certain episodes that may further clarify the meaning and development of the political events of those years.

All the troubles of the Party had begun in the spring of 1974, when the Professor had compelled his dubious friends to engage in a battle over the divorce referendum. This choice had been made after very long deliberations, during which two schools of thought had clashed. Some of his friends, led at the time by Deputy Moro, had felt it was necessary to reach an accord with the Left in order to pass a new divorce law and thus eliminate a useless and dangerous showdown with the voters. Others, led by the Professor, had been of the opinion that "this tooth ought to be pulled immediately," even at the cost of a test of strength.

But in addition to these two schools of thought, a third began to take shape. Many claimed to be undecided and professed themselves convinced that the Christian Democrat party was in a terrible dilemma. To reach an agreement with the Communists, it would have to pay too high a price, but if it did not, it would have to fight a battle whose results were highly uncertain. And some even dared to add, though in a whisper, that they were by no means persuaded that the Party would necessarily choose the lesser of two evils. Suppose the Party did not choose at all. After all, by a juridical quibble contrived by Moro's adviser Elia, it had already been possible to put off the referendum by a year, without anyone protesting. What a fine thing it would be, concluded these friends with a sigh, if Elia or some other jurist were to sharpen his wits still more and find a way to put off this damned referendum for a few more years. It wasn't possible? What a pity.

The Professor made his choice, and chose the worse path. The failure of that battle and the drubbing taken by the Party in local elections some months later nevertheless suggested to him a need for greater prudence. And when, in the autumn of that bitter 1974, a certain Tanassi, leader of the Social Democratic party, left the government coalition and rudely ordered the Professor to choose between him and a certain De Martino, leader of the Socialists, the Professor was very wary about pronouncing for one or the other.

Once again the discussions were long and animated, it being obvious that the Party could only lose by standing still in the middle of an Italy that every day was becoming more troubled and restless, while putting together governments capable of doing everything except governing. But the Professor knew how to maintain perfect control over his emotions. Nothing seemed to disturb him, not even the results of certain polls, secretly reported to him on the first Friday of every month. The Professor looked them over quickly, but his face, not yet adorned by the white beard, betrayed no sign of perturbation. He crammed the sheets in his pocket, went to church, solemnly heard mass, and stayed there for an hour on his knees, perhaps to pray, perhaps to meditate.

Unfortunately the already appreciable decline of the Party grew more rapid still. And this time it was certainly not the Professor's fault.

A few months before, one of the most stormy conclaves in the history of the Church had ended in Rome. Even at the beginning, two tendencies had emerged among the cardinals. The traditionalists inclined toward the election of another Italian, whereas the innovators wanted a foreigner, the better to testify to the universal mission of Catholicism. The innovators were in the majority but were unable to agree on who should ascend to the papal throne. The Americans supported the archbishop of Boston, highly popular among the Irish community, or as a second choice the archbishop of Dublin. But arrayed against these innovators from the rather backward cultural hinterland were the Dutch, and they were joined by many cardinals of different nationalities who shared, however, a common progressive theological stance. The Dutch might even have won had they been able to attain the assent of the Third World representatives, who maintained, however, that the universal mission of the Church would never emerge with the proper clarity if the conclave did not come up with an African pope, or, failing that, an Asian one. But the Dutch drew back, convinced that the theological stance of the Third World representatives might have some surprises in store. Further complicating these alignments were the Latin American cardinals, half superconservatives and half superprogressives, and the Italians themselves, by now powerless to elect a pope of their own, but sufficiently numerous to overturn any majority by exploiting the rivalry that had broken out among the foreigners.

The cardinals stayed locked up for seventy-three days before the puff of white smoke announced the election. And as had almost always happened in such cases, the papal throne was ascended by a cardinal to whom no one so far had given any thought: a German, who salvaged the principle of a foreign pope, but a tranquil German, very advanced in years, just the man to reassure both the Americans and the cardinals of the Curia. To tell the truth, no one knew what the new pope thought. To tell the whole truth, no one would ever know.

The new pope, who had assumed the name of Paul VII, had lived for a long time in the capital of Christianity, but that had been way back in the 1920s, when he was still a student in the seminary. After more than half a century of disuse, his mastery of the Italian language had obviously dimmed. Let me add that the new pope was unaware of his limits of expression, and besides, he had every wish to polish his Italian so as to establish warmer relations with the faithful who awaited his blessing in Saint Peter's Square.

The cardinals of the Curia and the high prelates had tried to obviate certain obstacles to expression by addressing Paul VII sometimes in French, sometimes in Latin, and more often in his mother tongue. But His Holiness had begged them to express themselves only in Italian. The cardinals had then tried to persuade him to choose a private secretary from the Rhineland or Thuringia, hoping in this way to smuggle in an interpreter. But Paul VII rejected this proposal with actual horror. Already the election of a foreign pontiff had been a traumatic experience for millions of Italian Catholics. Paul VII must do nothing, absolutely nothing, that might feed old prejudices and new suspicions. His closest collaborators all had to be Italians. The German pope, in the capital of Christianity, ought to seem the most Roman of them all.

Paul VII appeared every Sunday morning at a window of his Vatican residence to bless the faithful who crowded Saint Peter's Square. The new pope, however, had neither the hieratic voice of Pius XII and Paul VI, nor much less that warm and persuasive voice, with a slight Bergamo accent running through it, by which John XXIII had been able to arouse such emotion and enthusiasm. Paul VII expressed, or rather meant to express, the noblest concepts and the highest thoughts, but he mangled all the words. No German can know how comical his accent seems to an Italian the minute he tries to express himself in the language of Dante. And, unfortunately, Paul VII was no exception.

From the height of his balcony His Holiness observed that the crowd waiting for his blessing and message became denser every Sunday, and this filled him with joy and spurred him to persevere. He did not even imagine, the holy man, that the ranks of the devout, by now troubled and disappointed, had been replaced by impious groups of young hoodlums, ready to guffaw every time he made a blunder or mispronounced a word. And no one in the Vatican dared to explain the horrid reality to him. However, it would have been difficult to make him understand. His Holiness was also a little hard of hearing.

Television, which had contributed so much to the glory of previous popes, was this time forced to act as a sound box for misplaced accents. The directors had to broadcast, live, the ceremony in Saint Peter's Square, which to make matters worse had now gained a wide and appreciative audience. The fact is that they were obliged to contribute, against their own intentions and interests, to what was beginning to loom as a catastrophe for the Church and the Party. And for a few Sundays, no sooner had the cameramen trained their lenses on the solemn figure of the pontiff (being careful, however, not to take in the rowdy young hoodlums) than all the television sets in Italy began to gasp and whine. The usual announcement appeared on the screen: "The broadcast will be resumed as soon as possible." But the picture came back on only when the pope, having finished reading his message, was imparting the *urbi et orbi* blessing.

Whoever had invented this ingenious expedient had not, however, taken into account the fact that television had also changed, that the old owl of the monopoly had been transformed into a two-headed owl. The truth was that the so-called reform of the RAI-TV* (the only one passed in those years) had been launched amid general indifference, the Italians having suspected only one more device for canvassing votes. And up to now the two news broadcasts, the Catholic one on the first channel and the lay one on the second, had seemed

* Italian state radio and television network; its emblem is an owl. (Tr.)

equally dull. But as soon as the Catholics on Channel 1 began to censor the ceremony in Saint Peter's Square, the laymen on Channel 2 began to transmit it in color.

Their great success with the public drove the laymen to still more reckless enterprises. Alighiero Noschese, an actor and skillful mimic of important personalities, was hired. Noschese appeared on the news broadcast and read the Vatican bulletins and religious news items. He began in a soft and vaguely churchlike voice but suddenly pretended to get confused by imitating Paul VII's Teutonic accent. Unfortunately millions of Italians found his performance irresistible.

I will spare the reader an account (painful for me and tiresome for him) of all the vulgarities and indecencies that were encouraged by this revival of anticlericalism. I will only say that the filmmakers threw themselves into this new vein with avidity. Even the publishers went along: Podrecca's *Asino** was revived.

I cannot omit, however, the things that happened within the Church, and which had still more serious consequences for the Party.

All the cardinals who had clashed so violently during the recent conclave had done their utmost to impose their own theological views to the detriment of others, but none had thought to shatter that hierarchical principle by which Peter's successors had governed the Church for almost two thousand years. Even those who rejected, or at least pretended to ignore, the dogma of infallibility took care not to challenge the absolute authority of the Supreme Pontiff. It was up to him, and him alone, to resolve all controversies or mediate between

* Satirical, anticlerical magazine ("The Ass"), founded by Guido Podrecca in 1892 and suppressed by the Fascists in 1925. (Tr.)

differing opinions. He remained, for all the faithful, the precise point of reference, the guide to look to, Christ's Vicar on earth.

Instead, both innovators and traditionalists found themselves faced with a pope who spent the whole day combing the Zingarelli, the Palazzi, and even the very recent Melzi dictionaries. Paul VII, still convinced that his mission was to demonstrate that a German could be the most Roman of popes, refused to make any decisions. Perhaps for the first time in the history of the Church, a power vacuum had been created at the summit of the hierarchy.

The consequences were grave. If disorder ruled in the Vatican, chaos reigned in the parishes. If conflicts between tendencies raged in the Vatican, the high prelates giving themselves over to the most cynical power games, the confrontation in the parishes was equally furious. The exploits of Don Mazzi and Dom Franzoni* were now remembered with mild irony. Their successors were men of quite a different stamp, and furthermore they had realized that a pathetically ignorant pope and a divided and therefore impotent hierarchy would never oppose anything they might say, or anything they might do.

Radical priests became pugnacious to the point of arrogance. More important, all barriers disappeared between the orthodox and dissident clergy. As had already happened in the magistrates' courts, one could now find everything in the parishes as well, and certain young clerics, known as "assault priests," delivered sermons from the pulpit that to them seemed worthy of Savonarola, but to many of the faithful sounded blasphemous.

* The abbot Dom Franzoni was expelled from the Church for his left-wing views; Don Mazzi was a worker-priest in Florence. (Tr.)

Unconsciously, Paul VII had profaned the traditional image of the Supreme Pontiff, who ought to inspire reverence like Paul VI, or filial devotion like John XXIII, or even fear like Pius XII. Consciously, the radical priests had profaned the traditional image of the father-priest, whether he be sympathetic or severe. But the results had gone well beyond their intentions. In perceiving these shaggy, long-haired priests ascending the altars and imparting the sacred host, simple souls were seized by shivers of dismay. These outlandish-looking priests were unable to bring back anyone who had strayed from the faith, and succeeded in planting the germs of doubt in all the others. Many people, disgusted, began to look elsewhere. The Jehovah's Witnesses thrived. Even the Salvation Army gained legions of recruits.

What appeared as a disaster for the Church became a catastrophe for the Party. With two thousand years of history behind it, the Church could overcome even a power vacuum. Paul VII was old and the cardinals were already wondering who among themselves would be the most suitable for recovering the lost sheep. The Party, however, had the 1977 elections to face, and this religious crisis, added to the economic and political one, seemed like a *coup de grâce*. The most recent polls showed that the Communists, said to be planning to head the lists of leftist candidates, would in that case most certainly obtain fifty-two to fifty-seven per cent of the vote.

Merciless toward his dinner guests, but also toward himself, the Professor went on recalling all the vicissitudes of those terrible months and the long discussions with friends that had often lasted until morning. Even then, with disaster imminent, the two usual schools of thought had clashed again. Some had dusted off an old idea of Paolo Emilio Taviani, the Genoese political boss who just at that time had recovered, to his great satisfaction, the office of minister of the interior. For years Taviani had been saying, amid the skepticism of most people, that the Christian Democrats were by now a large secular party and that it would be just as well for them to keep their distance from the Church, which had become less a help than a hindrance.

Now the moment had come for the Party to hoist the Tavianian flag, flank it with the Professor's banner, and attempt to march forth from the besieged citadel, once again offering itself to the voters as the only political force capable of opposing the final triumph of communism. "True," argued the neo-Tavianians, "we're losing from ten to fifteen thousand voters a day, but that's only because the Party refuses to choose. So now let's choose."

Others instead asserted, with a wealth of sociological arguments, that the Italians were by now oriented toward the Left. Better therefore to make a deal with the Communists before it was too late, asking from their leader Berlinguer the stipulation of that historical compromise that he, in truth, no longer liked to speak of, but which he had never officially renounced.

But the Professor advanced another opinion. "Unfortunately," he exclaimed, "you're both right! Those who say that an election campaign just now would be madness are right, and so are those who say it's too late to sign the historical compromise. The elections are indeed upon us, and there's no need for Berlinguer to pay today for the power he can have tomorrow for nothing."

"And so?" asked the exponents of the two schools of thought, finally in unison. "We'll see," announced the Professor with an air of mystery. "We'll meet again in about three weeks, and at that time I hope to have something to tell you." I alone guessed, from certain words he had let drop, what the Professor was turning over in his mind. I alone knew he was thinking of those friends who back in 1972 had pointed out what a fine thing it would be if the date of the referendum, already postponed for one year, could be put off for still another and, God willing, forever.

At the time, betrayed by his combative spirit, the Professor had not cared to listen to that sound advice. But now, just when no one was bringing it up again, he was the only one to remember it.

Five days later, in Washington, the Professor and I found an unheard-of Kissinger, completely different from the calm and patient diplomat he had shown himself to be during his long negotiations with the Soviets and Chinese. The news from Ankara, from Belgrade, and from Madrid (which gave as a fact the advent to power by the left-wing military) had exasperated him. The news from Rome had enraged him. Kissinger received us rudely; it was all he could do to keep from hurling in the Professor's face a report delivered to him by the head of the CIA.

Nothing but insults issued from his mouth. The interpreter looked at him aghast, then turned to the Professor with an air of dismay, almost as though to beg his pardon; sometimes he lost the thread of the discourse and mumbled, hardly able to find the Italian equivalent for these furious imprecations, these terrible curses.

I must, however, acknowledge that to some extent the CIA report justified this outburst. The crisis in Italy was there painted in the gloomiest colors. The Communists were seen as sure winners in the coming elections, whereas the Christian Democrats would get no more than eighteen per cent of the vote. The economic crisis could not be halted, and the rate of inflation would go up from 42 to 116 per cent. According to a public-opinion poll ordered by the United States embassy in Rome, almost two million Italians, for the most part businessmen and professionals, were considering moving to Switzerland within two months. Another two million, almost all of them tradesmen, clerks, artisans, and even workers, intended to go to Australia, New Zealand, or South Africa. Of those who preferred to stay, sixty-five per cent wanted Berlinguer to take power, and believed him to be the only Italian still capable of restoring order to the country. Even with the dictatorship of the proletariat, if he thought it indispensable.

According to the CIA report, the Communists now controlled forty-seven per cent of the state prosecutors' offices of the Republic. High-level bureaucrats of the state, still formally loyal to the government, were negotiating with emissaries from the Communist party so as to pass over at the last moment to the side of the victors. The same could be said of the top editors of the newspapers, who were still pretending to defend the regime. The struggle between the factions in the Vatican continued to rage. The police and *carabinieri* were inefficient, to say the least. Ever since their right to organize themselves in unions had been recognized, they were on strike at least two days a week. The loyalty of the armed forces could not be counted on absolutely.

But it was not this information that had made Kissinger see red. What had driven him to invective had been, as we will see, a fatal coincidence. That CIA report, showing an Italy in coma, had landed on the secretary of state's desk simultaneously with a message from the Professor, asking if he might pay him a highly confidential visit to negotiate another loan, which would allow Italy finally to emerge from the tunnel of the crisis. "Let him come, let him come, *der liebe Professor!*" the secretary of state had exclaimed, sneering.

Now that the Professor was in his presence, Kissinger gave vent to his long-suppressed anger. "I'd just like to know," he shouted, "if you Italians consider us complete idiots. How do you have the nerve, the unmitigated gall, to ask me for a loan of four billion dollars on the eve of an election that you yourself are sure to be the first to lose? By what sort of logic do you pretend that the Congress of the United States will approve a loan that would only go to finance the Italian Communist party, a loan that would be all to the advantage of the Soviet Union?" Panting and red in the face, Kissinger paused. But it was in vain that he waited for a reaction from the Professor, who remained instead silent and imperturbable. Two interminable minutes went by. "But speak, at least say something," Kissinger blurted out, exasperated.

"I will, I will," answered the Professor. "My dear and illustrious friend, I only beg you to calm down. And let me tell you that from now on, if you so much as interrupt me, I won't say another word." Kissinger gave him a look that was both furious and awestruck. But the Professor was firm. "Do you promise?" "I promise," murmured Kissinger with a sigh. And he collapsed on the divan.

"First of all, I should like to remark," began the Professor, "that I haven't come to Washington at all to ask for four billion dollars. My intention has probably been misunderstood. Italy, I regret to say, needs a much more vigorous boost to emerge from the tunnel of the crisis: at least four billion dollars every six months, to be supplied over a period of time that, unfortunately, still can't be determined." Kissinger, by now exhausted, did not venture the slightest reaction.

"In the second place," continued the Professor, "I should like to remark that I certainly did not propose to cross the Atlantic to listen to a report on Italy's troubles, which I know as well, indeed better, than you. I should like to remark, in the third place, that the report you've given me is incomplete. And I myself will summarize, succinctly, what you've not thought it suitable to tell me.

"For instance, I think I can say that the American secret service has infiltrated our armed forces with many informers to determine the mood of our generals and find out if they have any intention of organizing a coup d'état. But your undercover agents could have spared themselves the time and trouble. Had they come to me, I would have explained to them in two words why a coup is impossible.

"It is impossible," the Professor went on sententiously, "for two reasons. First of all, the Italian army is technically incapable of carrying out a coup d'état. Even if no one talks about it, our military divisions are no less disorganized than our post offices. If some general should take it into his head to send a detachment to occupy a ministry, it would take two weeks for it to get to its destination.

"Besides, we have more than seven hundred generals, almost as many as we have senators and deputies. And our generals, no more and no less than our members of Parliament, have made their careers thanks to the protection of us politicians. Even in the army there are men loyal to Moro, to Andreotti, to Taviani, to Piccoli, and some are personally loyal to me. Just recently many friends of the Socialists have also emerged, and even of Berlinguer. A coup, already impossible technically, has thus become politically superfluous. As it is, the general staff reflects the composition of Parliament and would end by expressing the same political pattern. The struggle between tendencies would go on. With a single difference: we would have armed tendencies."

Now the Professor was spilling forth his arguments in the certainty of not being interrupted. "We are well aware, my dear and illustrious friend, that you Americans have also taken soundings in the opposite direction. Your contacts with the Italian Communists, confidential to be sure but not really all that secret, have been going on for some time. But allow me to say that in this case you Americans are committing a gross error in evaluation.

"And not, as fools think, because the Italian Communist party is too tied to the Soviet Union, not because the Italian Communist party is only a slightly disguised copy, substantially modeled on that CPSU that your Kremlinologists know so well. No, you have made the opposite mistake: you have never realized just how Italian the party led by Deputy Berlinguer really is. My dear and illustrious friend, the Italian Communists are much more similar to us than to their Soviet comrades. As I can easily demonstrate. Did you ever in the course of your soundings find anyone who answered you with a firm yes or a firm no? Out of all those conversations, you've acquired nothing but a collection of 'neithers,' just as when you talk with us Christian Democrats. Have you ever succeeded in understanding what kind of government they want to form, what kind of system they want to build, once they've achieved power? Have you ever understood just what they mean by their new model of development? They've always been cautious and vague, just like us Christian Democrats.

"Have you ever succeeded in understanding what their historical compromise means? What their real relations with the Soviet Union are? Are they in accord? Do they think they're in accord? Do they pretend to be in accord? Or else do they pretend not to be in accord? I'll bet you've sometimes tried to sound out Brezhnev himself. And I'll bet Brezhnev answered, 'If only I knew!' "

The Professor appeared in better form than I had ever seen him. Once he had gathered momentum, no one could stop him. "At your age, my dear and illustrious friend, I too had a fiery nature. The burden of years has led me to greater calm. I lose my temper only when I hear it said, by certain fools or hypocrites, that the Italian Communists are serious people. They, serious people? Maybe because they never laugh? They, serious people? But even if it's true, why should the Christian Democrats be buffoons? The fact is that we Christian Democrats and the Communists are twin brothers. We coin the same high-sounding and incomprehensible slogans; we issue the same prolix, tortuous, and ambiguous statements; we weave the same complicated political plots, without carrying any of them out to the end. We have the same nostalgia for the past and the same fear of the future. We are in terror of leaving the government; they are in terror of arriving at the government. In this too we are united. We are two sides of the same coin. And neither we nor they have any intention of playing heads-or-tails."

Kissinger managed to speak up. "But now the moment has come to play. The elections take place in a few months."

"Mr. Kissinger, never mind the elections. The real subject we have to discuss is something else. How much is the United States obliged to pay—excuse me, to lend—if only to keep the present Center-Left political structure alive? We consider that a semiannual loan of four billion dollars, at three per cent annual interest and indefinitely renewable, would be enough to keep this framework from going to pieces. And if the United States is ready to accept and honor this task, I guarantee you that from now on Italy will do likewise."

"And the elections?" murmured Kissinger in a small voice.

"I'm telling you for the last time, never mind the elections. And for the last time I say: are you willing or not? Yes or no? You haven't become a Communist or Christian Democrat yourself, have you?"

The interpreter stumbled a little over some of the Professor's Tuscan diction, comprehensible only in the area around Arezzo, but Kissinger was able all the same to perceive the transaction that had been proposed to him. Still skeptical but amused, he exclaimed: "Oh, all right, if you can keep to what you've said, I agree. I promise."

Poor man, he had no idea of the troubles that lay in store for him.

At exactly midnight the evening of our return from America, the Professor and I, scarves over our faces, the collars of our overcoats turned up, wide-brimmed hats pulled down over our eyes, set out from Piazza del Gesù and walked the short distance to Via delle Botteghe Oscure, where the headquarters of the Communist party was then located. Three times we pressed the bell of the service entrance. The door was opened by Antonino Tatò, and as always we embraced. In our youth, Tonino and I had been active among the Catholic Communists. Over the years, Tonino had become all Communist, I all Catholic, but we had remained friends.

After our embrace, Tatò stuck his head out the door and with an impatient nod motioned the Professor, who was waiting on the sidewalk, to come in. In that gesture I once again saw all the old Tonino. Ever since his earliest youth he had always loved conspiracies and secret meetings.

We followed Tonino, who was carrying a flashlight, up to the floor above, where Berlinguer, along with his most trusted comrades, was waiting for us. Berlinguer made a sign to Tonino to leave, while the Professor ordered me to stay. Tonino and I exchanged a swift look of understanding. I would certainly tell him everything the following day.

"You see before you," began the Professor, "the general of a defeated army. A general who has come only to hand over his sword and negotiate the terms of surrender."

"But the elections are still three months away!" exclaimed Giancarlo Pajetta. "Since when does a general negotiate surrender before the final battle?" But the Professor pretended not to hear, and Berlinguer gave Pajetta an icy look.

"I've come to propose," the Professor went on, "three different surrender treaties. I'm ready to endorse, on behalf of my party as well, that 'historical compromise' which you yourself, Deputy Berlinguer, were promoting back in 1973. But I realize that it is highly improbable that it can be negotiated and concluded with the elections so close at hand. I am ready, also on behalf of my party, to face the battle of the elections, pledging myself to conduct an orderly and civilized campaign, with no party strife and no crusading overtones, since I know very well that it would now be impossible to upset the result. Nor need you fear any last last-minute surprises on our part: the elections will take place in a regular manner. And as soon as the voters' response is known, you can be sure that the president, for the first time in the history of the Republic, will entrust a Communist with the task of forming a government.

"I know that the job will go to you, Deputy Amendola," added the Professor, smiling. "Allow me to offer you all the good wishes you deserve, all the more since you'll have need of them. It was you, back in 1973, who expressed some apprehension about the seriousness of the problems a leftist bloc would have to face if it were called upon to govern Italy. And if this was true at that time, when Italy was a flourishing and prosperous country, how much truer it will be today, in the conditions to which Italy has been reduced."

"The conditions to which you've reduced it," retorted Deputy Amendola. But from the resentful, almost angry tone of his reply, one could see that Amendola had by no means got over his fear of governing.

The moment had come to explain the third surrender

proposal. "Dear friends—you'll allow me, won't you, to call you friends?—I know very well that Deputy Amendola isn't the only one who's worried. Italy seems to be in a coma, and at this point it's not important to know who has reduced it to that. What we are concerned with is something else. The new doctor who will shortly be called to the bedside knows that from now on his job is impossible. The patient cannot be cured, he can only be kept alive; and the doctor is not even able to guarantee his survival. Once he approaches the bedside, he will in fact find himself without medicine, which, as you know better than I, means international aid.

"To a patient in such serious condition, even the slightest change could be fatal. And if we were in a hospital, I'm sure you and I would immediately find ourselves in agreement. But neither you nor I are doctors. Unfortunately, we are politicians, and I know you certainly won't draw back, now that you're on the point of taking power. All the more since power is lying on the floor, and all you have to do is bend over and pick it up.

"But why not leave it lying there? Why not pick it up at a more opportune moment? Who's going to touch it? Who are you afraid of? Certainly not of us, who have now become the skeleton of what was once a great party and are condemned to lose still more importance and prestige."

Berlinguer and his comrades looked at him with stony faces. Obviously they had still not understood what the Professor was driving at.

"In your interests and ours, and above all in the higher interests of the Italian people, I've had another idea. At times it seems to me absurd, other times it seems to me the most sensible idea ever to come into my head during my political career. If it is true that it would not be expedient to move the patient, then why move him? If it would be expedient to all of us to perpetuate, I'd almost say freeze, the present political situation, then why not freeze it? If, and let's put it frankly, these elections, which would shift the present equilibriums too drastically, are expedient to no one, then who is forcing us to challenge each other in an election campaign? It was you yourselves, on the eve of the divorce referendum, who proposed a bargain to me that would have avoided, or at least postponed, that useless showdown whose results were so disastrous. I was so stupid as not to accept. Now I wouldn't like to see you make the same mistake.

"And don't come and tell me it can't be done. If you and we are in agreement, we can do anything in this country. The Constitution won't allow it? But together we can change it when we like. If these elections are to be put off, they'll be put off. If they aren't to be held, they won't be held.

"Who's going to object? Certainly not the neo-Fascists, who would be immediately outlawed if you assumed power. Certainly not the Social Democrats, who've been thinking of moving their party offices to Switzerland. Not the Socialists, who say they're always in agreement with you, but prefer by far to be in the government with us. The freeze is useful to everyone, including Leone, who will obviously see his term of office extended.

"The pact I'm offering you," concluded the Professor, "seems to me honest and loyal. I'd call it the 'little historical compromise,' since it's much less ambitious than the one that you, Deputy Berlinguer, once had the kindness to suggest, but it's much easier to carry out. It's a natural pact between two parties that remain adversaries, but in these circumstances have everything to gain and nothing to lose.

"You, Deputy Pajetta," continued the Professor, "were

perhaps about to add that we Christian Democrats are the only ones with anything to gain. Allow me to disagree. If it is true, as you yourselves once recognized, that the Left cannot govern Italy with fifty-one percent of the vote, well, wait for it to increase. If it is true, as we are the first to recognize, that for years you have been infiltrating the courts, the state bureaucracy, the armed forces, well, go on infiltrating so that what will happen tomorrow, without shocks, without traumas, and without bloodshed, will not only be a change of government but an overthrow of the system. If it is true, as you recognize as well as we, that the Italians would have nothing to live on without international aid, well, why do you want to take over the government and force Italy's friends to suspend such aid? How, in that case, would you get the Italians to survive? With Soviet rubles? Or with Soviet tanks?"

Berlinguer turned to the door. Tonino came in with a pot of coffee. While Tatò was pouring coffee for the Professor and the writer of these notes, Berlinguer made a sign to his comrades, summoning them to the back of the room. They spoke for a while in low voices, like basketball players during the minute of time out.

Then Berlinguer came back to the Professor and said: "We've decided to take surrender proposal number three under consideration. We'll let you know our final decision the day after tomorrow."

Then the Professor announced the "little historical compromise" and the indefinite postponement of the elections to the leaders of the Party, there was a moment of bewildered surprise, followed by a very long burst of applause. Everyone wanted to embrace him. Donat Cattin and Paolo Emilio Taviani, his stanchest enemies, wanted to kiss his hand.

But as soon as it became certain that it would be possible to go on governing for heaven knows how much longer, with American dollars and the consent of the Communists, those damned two customary schools of thought were re-established. The leader of the first school was Mariano Rumor, who, after a brief period of eclipse, was once again gaining influence and prestige. Until the middle of the 1970s, Rumor had been one of the central figures in Italian political life, and he had obtained this power less for his qualities than for certain calculations as irrefutable as a theorem.

An alliance between Right and Left being inconceivable, the Christian Democrats, by placing themselves at the center of the political spectrum, had the certainty of being part of any government. The Christian Democrats were in turn divided into eight factions, and to the faction of the Dorotei,* which had placed itself at the center of the Party, naturally went the most important ministries. Mariano Rumor, who had placed

* So named for having held meetings in a convent of Dorothean nuns in 1959 when the various tendencies within the Christian Democrat party became crystallized into factions. (Tr.)

himself at the center of the Dorotei faction, was therefore the natural pretender to the office of prime minister.

These geometric designs were upheld by equally precise mathematical calculations. The Christian Democrats had the right to head every government coalition, being the party with a relative majority, that is to say the one that got the greatest number of votes in elections. The Dorotei had the right to the most important ministries because they were the faction with a relative majority within the party with a relative majority. Mariano Rumor aspired to the office of prime minister because, within the Dorotei faction, it was he who controlled the strongest group. In short, Rumor had been head of the government five times because he had at his disposal the group with a relative majority within the faction with a relative majority in the party with a relative majority.

When, in the middle of 1974, the Center-Left political framework began cracking, Mariano Rumor had set himself apart in lordly fashion, accepting ministries of notable prestige but certainly not corresponding to his importance. But now that the framework had been put back in order, Mariano Rumor was returning to reclaim his rights.

If the little historical compromise, ingeniously achieved by the Professor, made it possible to freeze the disposition of Parliament, Rumor did not see why those criteria should not also be respected by which ministerial offices had up till then been distributed. Certain political structures could not be restored without meanwhile also establishing order and harmony within these structures.

The adherents of the second school of thought were much more numerous. Conspicuous among them were Andreotti, a Roman, right-hand man of the Curia as long as the Vatican had counted for something; Ciriaco De Mita, dynamic and unscrupulous boss of Avellino; and Aldo Moro, the only Christian Democrat who had swallowed the little historical compromise with reluctance, since he had been hoping to succeed Leone in the Quirinale. The rebels were also joined by Donat Cattin, a Piedmontese and rebel by definition, detested by all but likewise feared.

Giulio Andreotti and Aldo Moro, by far the most influential and informed exponents of the second group, brought arguments to bear on Rumor that were no less convincing. The stability of the political framework was one thing; quite another were the absurd criteria by which Rumor claimed to interpret the little historical compromise, which they themselves also firmly supported. It was by appealing to the happy experiences of the past that Rumor had fallen into the most striking contradictions. Just at that time, when the framework had appeared so stable as to seem eternal, there had been a constant and salutary exchange: of men, of ideas, of groups, of factions. In those happy times, no government had ever lasted more than a year. "One must make a distinction," argued Moro, "between the irreversibility of the Center-Left, of which I myself have been a stubborn and prophetic champion, and the irreversibility of Center-Left governments, which to the best of my ability I have always tried to demolish."

It was clear that the struggle between the Dorotei and the other factions would be a furious one. Rumor was adamant: posts and offices must be distributed according to the geometrical and mathematical criteria he had listed, and there was to be no more talk about it until such time as the Professor and the Communists had decided on new elections. Andreotti and Moro instead maintained that Rumor and his followers no longer any right to claim the most prestigious offices, since their electoral constituencies, on which they had once based their power, had either melted or were melting away. Andreotti and Moro were the first to recognize that they too found themselves in the same situation as Deputy Rumor. And so? Since the starting point was the same for all, one might just as well set up criteria for rotation.

The dissidents proposed forming a new government every six months, so that first all the leaders of factions, then all the leaders of groups, might in turn have the satisfaction of occupying the office of prime minister. Put to a vote, this thesis prevailed, but other, no less furious struggles developed in order to establish how the rotation should be regulated. To whom should the post of head of the government go first, and to whom last?

Rumor had the happy intuition to seize on a moment of general weariness and propose a second vote, in which he was easily the winner. A week later he had already formed his sixth cabinet. All the experts wrote that this government would stay in office for the entire duration of the little historical compromise. Which is to say, quite a while.

But never were the predictions of journalists to be so resoundingly, or rather tragically, refuted as they were this time.

Hardly two weeks later, Mariano Rumor was found dead in his bed by the servant who had come in as always at nine in the morning with coffee, milk, bread, butter, and jam. The doctor diagnosed a heart attack and authorized his burial. The funeral rites were celebrated at state expense. Representatives of all parties in the constitutional spectrum delivered heartfelt and moving speeches. All the newspapers, those leaning toward the government as well as those inspired by the opposition, published long articles recalling the honesty, the gifts of balance and moderation, and the sincere democratic sentiments of the Deceased.

The government crisis was resolved with lightning speed. Leone entrusted the job to Flaminio Piccoli, a close friend of the deceased who reassembled the same government, in homage to the man to whom, as he said himself, he had been roped like a mountain climber. But unfortunately the Piccoli government, for which everyone prophesied long life, was also destined not to last. The new prime minister, who had gone to his native Trentino to spend a weekend, was found as a corpse at the bottom of a ravine. His chest had been pierced by his trusty mountaineering pick, inseparable companion of so many such excursions.

The cruel fate that seemed to pursue the most influential Dorotei did not keep Antonio Bisaglia (Toni to his friends) from accepting Leone's invitation and forming a new government, in every way resembling the previous ones. But, two weeks later, he too had to give up his office, and in truly horrifying circumstances.

Whenever he went to his native Rovigo, Toni Bisaglia loved to distill, from carefully selected grape dregs, an aqua vitae that, besides serving the needs of his family, was sent every Christmas to his dearest friends and most dangerous enemies. This liquor, dry and sweet at the same time, aroused unanimous approval, and had been of no small help to Toni from the beginning, when he had still to make his way among the Christian Democrat party notables of the Veneto. But what had been the basis for a bright and dazzling career also became the cause of woeful events. While the new prime minister, on his return from mass, was busying himself around his still, the neighbors heard a terrific explosion. All help was unavailing: Toni's mangled body was found among the grape dregs.

Paolo Emilio Taviani, urged by Leone to assume the job, decided to take his time. The conflict in his mind was moreover understandable. Taviani was the only political boss of the so-called second generation of Christian Democrats who had never succeeded in becoming head of the government, and therefore Leone's offer, albeit tardy, had not left him indifferent. On the other hand, the sudden deaths of three prime ministers in less than two months made a certain caution seem advisable.

Not unskillfully, Taviani persuaded Leone to entrust him with an exploratory assignment that would allow him to survey the lay of the land before giving an answer. And while the explorer was receiving delegations from all parties, officials at the Ministry of the Interior began a discreet investigation of these accidents that were now too frequent to seem entirely fortuitous. But as fate would have it, poor Taviani was never to become prime minister. Shortly before receiving the Social Democratic delegation for the fourth time in two weeks, he was found dead in his bathtub.

This time it was impossible to attribute death to accidental causes. Poor Taviani had been found with his throat cut and a knife stuck between his third and fourth right ribs. The blood-soaked towels, the torn bathrobe, the bottle of lotion smashed on the floor showed that the victim had put up a vigorous struggle before succumbing to his assailant.

The police, spurred on by scathing editorials in the press, began to investigate small groups on the extreme Right and also on the extreme Left, but with no results. Its task, in itself already very difficult, actually became impossible when to the Taviani case a great number of others were suddenly added: all equally dreadful, all apparently inexplicable.

In two weeks twenty-seven politicians, all Christian Democrats, were murdered. People were particularly aroused by the photograph of Deputy Gullotti, his face hideously disfigured by a blast from a sawed-off shotgun. But the next day, Deputy Gioia, likewise a Sicilian, was kidnapped and tied to the railroad tracks. He was decapitated by the Palermo-Rome express. The public was also especially impressed by the death of Deputy Colombo, minister of the Treasury, who had taken advantage of a great many international engagements to stay on in Brussels. This precaution, however, turned out to be in vain. While Colombo was speaking at a conference on European inflation, a yawning and restless audience was jolted by the sound of a gunshot. Colombo lay on the floor, a bullet in his heart. Giulio Andreotti had taken refuge in the Vatican Library to finish work on a biography of Pius IX. An unknown person, disguised as a cardinal, had planted a knife in the middle of his chest as Andreotti was naïvely reaching out to kiss his ring.

The strategy of tension is beginning again, wrote the newspapers in anguish. No sooner had Italy succeeded in achieving stable governments, within a political framework that had finally been consolidated, than someone had gone back to weaving the most sinister and destructive plots. But not even this long Saint Bartholomew's Night, this chilling attempt physically to eliminate the most lucid brains of the political world, would do any good. Nothing by now could change the course of history.

The editorials in the daily papers were nevertheless refuted by still one more deed of blood. In a forest in Irpinia were found the corpses of two men who had been enemies for a long time, before killing each other in a ferocious rustic duel. They were Ciriaco De Mita, political boss of Avellino, and Fiorentino Sullo, former boss of the same city, whom De Mita had cynically deposed, forcing him to seek his fortune in the Social Democratic party. Two months before, Sullo had asked for and obtained re-entry into the Christian Democrat party in the hope of being able in his turn to expel his hated rival. But the settling of accounts had been fatal to both.

After this appalling but eloquent episode, no further doubt was possible. One could no longer speak of a long Saint Bartholomew's Night; it had become a long Saint Valentine's Day massacre. Like the Americans during their Prohibition era, the Christian Democrat bosses had thrown off their disguise.

Montecitorio* and Villa Madama had remained the only two oases of (relative) peace in all Rome. Senators and deputies had pledged themselves to respect the dignity of Parliament and leave their weapons in the vestibule. But the Montecitorio taproom, once the scene of so many circumspect and critical conversations, now looked like a saloon. Those who up to now had been known for their ceremonious smiles, their slight bows, their soft, light, but prolonged handshakes, now walked with a ribald air and with their chests thrown out. Half drunk on whisky, the bosses insulted one another in loud voices and challenged one another to duels.

It was obvious that the most influential spokesmen for the Party had lost their common sense, and it was not too difficult to explain why. These friends, now engaged in deadly feuds, had passed too quickly from extreme euphoria to extreme prostration. The little historical compromise, the prospect of administering power indefinitely with American dollars and Communist consent, had rekindled hopes once faded, dreams that had seemed forbidden. But then when least expected, Rumor had come along with his Euclidean geometry and Pythagorean tables to insist that the best offices should go only, and for all time, to himself and his faithful followers.

The others, aware of their own impotence but incapable of resigning themselves to endless parliamentary anonymity, had seen red. Rumor and Piccoli had certainly been murdered, but with a certain ingenuity so that their deaths might seem acci-

* The seat of Parliament. (Tr.)

dental. The conspirators still hoped that the Dorotei would understand and see reason, by coming to accept the principle of ministerial rotation. The atrocious death of Bisaglia had been an ultimatum. In the newspapers it had still been attributed to natural causes, but the experts could no longer have any illusions. And when poor Taviani, despite the ultimatum, had continued to shilly-shally, the plotters had come out in the open by killing him in the bath. From then on it had been war. And the Dorotei had picked up the gauntlet. An eye for an eye, a tooth for a tooth.

"You see," the Professor said to me, "this is a difficult moment for the Party. By now all our friends are thirsting for revenge, and all of them have someone to avenge. All we can do is resign ourselves to the course of events. I cannot intervene. Better to keep out of it while the shooting is going on. When the brawlers have used up their ammunition, then the peacemaker can step forward."

Nor did the Professor seem overly alarmed. "You're wrong," he kept telling me. "The Center-Left political framework will go on holding. The Americans and Communists don't really care if the Christian Democrat deputies slaughter one another. For them it's enough that the dead be replaced, and so far that's always happened. Not even the Italians seem to me upset or daunted by it. Twenty-seven corpses in two months are too many; it's no longer news. The last two undersecretaries killed the other day ended up on the inside pages of the newspapers. All I'm wondering is this: if the shootings go on, will Leone still find anyone willing to form a government? That's all that worries me. I wouldn't like to see the Americans and Communists lose patience in the face of a power vacuum."

The solution was found by Moro, who had emerged alive but not unscathed from the long Saint Valentine's Day massacre. His left cheek had been slashed by a knife, giving his face a more virile if sinister look. His hip had been struck by a sniper's bullet, and this made him walk with a halting, but also vaguely martial, step.

Above all, the would-be assassins had transformed that once cautious and elusive man into a hard and practical one. The physique of an old pirate was combined with a macho vocabulary: "Professor, old boy, if the two of us don't put a stop to it, these dumb bastards will end up killing themselves off. The less important they are, the more they want to be big shots. You say nothing can be done, but I've had an idea. Let's make up our minds, and the war will be over tomorrow. Let's leave these dumb bastards with their ass in a sling."

Expressed in less picturesque terms, Moro's idea was as follows: The president was to choose a prime minister from outside Parliament, without abrogating the right of the two chambers to approve or reject his decision by a vote. The senators and deputies, exhausted by the fratricidal struggle, would now ratify any presidential choice that allowed them to put an end to their duels. Everyone would be satisfied not to see his rivals prevail.

And so it was. The job was given to Ruggero Bertolon, a farm owner from the Vicenza countryside. His ministers, one per region, were drawn by lots from the membership of the Christian Democrat party. No one objected, and the solidity of the political framework was once again assured.

The shootings immediately became less frequent, but never entirely ceased. At least once a month the police discovered the corpse of some former undersecretary in an alleyway in the old section of Rome.

These were not the only troubles, in any case more extravagant than serious, that the little historical compromise had provoked. Quite something else were the difficulties that threatened to undermine the agreement barely reached between Berlinguer and the Professor. Difficulties less striking, but infinitely more dangerous.

By deciding to take surrender proposal number three under consideration, the Communists had committed a grave error in judgment. Lama, the secretary of the CGIL,* had promised full union support for the Communist party initiative, but this assurance was soon seen to have been rash. The trade unionists, caught off guard, had at first raised no objections, but after a few days it dawned on them that the Kissinger-Professor-Berlinguer agreement was serious and perhaps lasting, such as rapidly to erode all the influence and power they had acquired in recent years, at the cost of harsh struggle.

Above all, the most influential representatives of the CISL**—Storti, Macario, and Pierre Carniti—were of the same opinion. Since the Professor was now in agreement with Berlinguer and ready to do anything the latter asked, the trade unionists of the CISL would soon find themselves out of the game, unable either to put pressure on the government or take a polemical, or simply dialectical, stand against the party that

* Confederazione Generale Italiana del Lavoro, Italian General Confederation of Labor; Communist-oriented. (Tr.)
** Confederazione Italiana Sindacati Lavoratori, Italian Confederation of Trade Union Workers; oriented toward the Christian Democrats. (Tr.)

still enjoyed the full confidence of the workers. For a few days, Storti, Macario, and Pierre Carniti had the actual sensation of finding themselves squeezed in a vise. But at the last moment they were able to escape this fatal grip.

Kissinger, the Professor, and Berlinguer had in fact worked out a plan that seemed perfect, and instead was only nearly perfect. Kissinger had been too generous, the Professor and the Communists too demanding. Those eight billion dollars a year, which would in any case have prevented the final collapse of the Italian economy, offered the trade unionists of the CISL a hitherto unhoped-for margin for maneuver.

It was Storti, in his retreat at Cortina d'Ampezzo, who launched the counteroffensive. Born in Rome, and thus a profound expert on the civil service, Storti had a particular feeling for what public employees understood by a "new model of development." They would adapt themselves easily even to a more modest standard of living, virtuously renouncing all the allurements of the consumer society, if the trade union were to guarantee them in exchange an adequate margin of free time to compensate them for these sacrifices. It was Storti, in short, who was the first to introduce that procedure later called by the sociologists "full disengagement." This practice, immediately accepted by civil servants in the South, was soon adopted, though with some resistance, in the industrial North.

Tireless as always, Storti and his comrades went from one meeting to another. They took care not to challenge the little historical compromise, and confined themselves to asking that it be correctly interpreted. Reasonable and even accommodating about wage claims, they became intransigent about work rules and regulations, proposing new labor methods to the captains of industry. Only after two weeks of negotiations was Fiat able to obtain a three-week work contract, if only to set back in motion the assembly lines that were threatening to rust. And this was accomplished with the discreet support of the Communists. Cefis alone, as we know, had resolved his production problems by minting gold coins and getting the help of the Gurkhas, but Storti and his friends were wise enough not to bother him. Indeed, relations between Storti and Cefis, founded on mutual noninterference in each other's internal affairs, were unfailingly good. The two were seen many times going hunting together on an estate near Pavia on the other side of the Po River.

There was no lack of people nostalgic for the old order, ready to exclaim every morning that Italy had touched bottom and that "it was no longer possible to go on like this." In reality, the Italians demonstrated that they could go on fairly well, though in their own way.

True, traffic was paralyzed, through both the absolute insufficiency of public transport and the scarcity of private automobiles, but a pleasant neighborhood life flourished as compensation. Children played ball in the street, men played cards on the sidewalk, women knitted or crocheted in the doorways of the houses. True, the streets of the center in every city were forever invaded by mobs of young hoodlums wearing red kerchiefs, and these gangs stopped automobiles and sometimes exacted a toll from cyclists and even pedestrians. But it seldom went beyond that. Their actions did not keep sufficient pace with their virulence of language and their quarrelsome and sometimes provocative attitudes. Though these youths were overloaded with chains and iron bars, serious incidents were nonetheless rare. Clashes and skirmishes were frequent but took place according to a kind of code of honor respected by everyone. No one would have taken advantage of anyone who had fallen to the ground or who raised an arm in a sign of surrender.

The massive importation of Gurkhas had stifled the activities of the anonymous kidnappers. Bank robberies were also less numerous, since the profession itself had become more difficult. Automobiles being scarce, it was not always easy to steal one, and a roadblock improvised in the street to exact a toll could get the bandits in trouble. Besides, inflation had eroded the value of banknotes, and it was now both troublesome and dangerous to pile bushel baskets full of paper currency into a car. On the other hand, brawls were continually increasing, especially at closing time in the bars, as well as so-called crimes of honor. Too much free time, said the sociology professors.

Telephones functioned little and poorly; the postal services did not function at all. Industries, ministerial and party offices, and the trade unions themselves now used private couriers. But then the situation was no worse than when public employees had gone regularly to their offices.

True, industrial production, except for the petrochemical sector, seemed on the brink of collapse. The Fiat group, for example, was unable to extract more than three or four work contracts a year from the trade unions. In the immense Mirafiori lots in Turin, where automobiles had once been stored after emerging from the assembly lines, volleyball tournaments, roller-skating contests, and especially beach-ball competitions now took place. In the industrial belt around Milan, where space was more limited, bowling was very popular.

True, pessimists had the upper hand in demonstrating that the volume of industrial production was equal to that of 1944 during the German occupation, but even the optimists could register some points in their favor. Agricultural production had increased in the meantime, even if no immigrant in the North had returned to his village in the South. Many young foreigners, especially Americans and Scandinavians, had come to Italy and set themselves up in the uncultivated countryside. They professed to be attracted by the mild climate, the beauty of the landscape, and the purity of the air. The pollution level in Italy was by now very low indeed, only slightly higher than that recorded for Tibet, Bolivia, and Saudi Arabia. These young people, lovers of nature and rustic life, ended by producing more than enough for their own needs, and naturally they started selling, at reasonable prices, their extra tomatoes, potatoes, and pigs.

And if industry languished, handicrafts flourished again. Not all workers spent their free time bowling or playing cards. Many, once freed from the assembly line or the office manager, had rediscovered a taste for certain skills that had been the pride of their ancestors. Now by the roadsides they displayed agreeable objects in wrought iron, pleasing wooden sculptures, straw hats and bags, splendid tablecloths hand-embroidered by their women. In the growing number of tourist groups they found a sure clientele.

But in this somewhat anarchic, somewhat Arcadian Italy, really not so bad as we might imagine today with our mentality of the year 2000, there was something that was not going well at all. The more relations between the Christian Democrats and Communists improved, the more relations between the Communists and trade unions worsened. Tonino spoke to me about it one day, and it was he who confided to me that Berlinguer was very worried.

"The Center-Left," Berlinguer was in the habit of repeating, "has had three phases. The first, from 1962 to 1968, was characterized by the dominant position of the Christian Democrats. Our opponents weren't strong enough to govern by themselves, but they were still strong enough to persuade the Socialists to break off relations with us and to relegate us to a position of complete isolation. As you well know, our opponents did not succeed.

"The second phase runs from 1968 to 1977. Confrontation between the Christian Democrats and our party lasted a good nine years, a confrontation that took place with a series of ups and downs. The Christian Democrats, now incapable of isolating us, tried to relegate us to the margins of power, that is to say they fought for their privileges by putting up a defensive battle, skillfully conducted but lacking imagination. During this period our capacity to apply pressure was progressively increased, and from the beginning of the 1970s on, no law was ever passed by Parliament over the opposition of us Communists. And we could state, with legitimate pride: no one rules the government against the Communists, no one rules the government without the Communists. It was the simple truth.

"A few months ago the third and last phase of the Center-Left began. Since we considered it premature, and therefore dangerous, to take over the administration of power, we willingly listened to the requests of our opponents and agreed to postpone the political elections. But from now on it's clear that we must begin to govern the country. If up until yesterday no law was passed without our consent, from today on only those laws will pass that we ourselves formulate and want. If up until yesterday you could say that no one governed without the Communists, from today on people should know that only the Communists agree to govern. And when the economy has been adjusted, when a minimum of order has been re-established, when the great majority of Italians have abandoned all their prejudices and suspicions concerning us and have realized that we're indispensable for the salvation and prosperity of the nation, then the third phase will also end. With no shocks or traumas for anyone, we will then take over."

But even for Berlinguer, this was easier said than done. The Communist leader was not particularly concerned about Storti and Pierre Carniti, whom he considered irksome but not overly important; on the other hand, he was alarmed by their unforeseen allies. With all the influence he still had on the workers, Berlinguer should have been confident of first containing, then reabsorbing, the anarchic impulses provoked by certain reckless demagogues. Instead he felt completely powerless in the face of a new situation that had arisen.

By now they all recognized it: it had been a serious mistake, the year before, to insist on setting up a trade union among the police and *carabinieri,* so as to deprive the Christian Democrats of even the last separate body over which they still exercised a certain control. The initiative had indeed been successful, but unfortunately the success was much greater than had been foreseen.

The Communists had thought that these poor lads, obliged to live a wretched and dangerous life for starvation wages, would free themselves with enthusiasm from a set of rules that were by now more archaic and severe than even the prison regulations. But they could never have imagined that in only a few weeks these same poor lads would be capable of doing a complete about-face. And with a bitterness equaled only by their astonishment, they realized that the first speeches by their delegates in the barracks were greeted with only polite applause, whereas the representatives of the CISL received actual ovations.

Before the Central Committee had time to formulate a new political line toward the forces of law and order, the CISL had already signed up seventy-eight per cent of the police and eighty-two per cent of the *carabinieri,* pledging itself to support all their demands: no limitation on the right to strike; a thirty-six-hour work week; the refusal to intervene, for any reason and under any circumstances, against demonstrations organized by democratic and progressive forces; direct election of commissioned and noncommissioned officers.

Finally, Berlinguer had neglected to propose the disarming of the police forces, expecting to raise this second demand on a later occasion. This excess of caution was likewise to prove a tragic error. Now that the police and *carabinieri* had become the most progressive forces in Italian democracy, it was obviously impossible to propose disarming them. Not even Berlinguer could lightheartedly lay himself open to the accusation of playing the reactionaries' game and encouraging a coup d'état.

The Communists had had to resign themselves to seeing circulate in the streets of all Italian cities squads of police and *carabinieri* who protected public order in a special—an all too special—manner. The first paragraph of their new regulations, voted by acclamation, said that the primary task of the police forces was to protect the weak against the will of the strong, but this sentence, obvious in itself, lent itself to the most deft and extended interpretations.

The weak, for example, included those gangs of young hoodlums who by now occupied the center of every Italian city, setting up or dismantling roadblocks as they pleased, and forcing the passersby to purchase their little newspapers or even sign up for a subscription. Also among the weak were those groups who had installed permanent roadblocks on all the bridges of the Tiber in order to collect tolls. Weak, indeed very weak, were the Vigilantes who had invaded the gardens of the Quirinale, compelling Leone to repair discreetly to Villa Madama. As well as those demonstrators who had forced Kissinger to land by helicopter on the field of the Olympic Stadium.

Berlinguer, who still had the confidence of the working class and therefore could not be ousted on the Left, was forced to accept everything. The third phase, so carefully planned, was turning out to be a disaster. Just at the moment when his chief adversary had negotiated surrender, Berlinguer was incapable of making the most of his triumph. Just when the Professor and his friends would have diligently carried out all his orders, Berlinguer found himself in the situation of submitting to any folly that came into the heads of a group of unbridled demagogues.

Such had been the last years of our history: from May 12, 1974, to January 12, 1980. Naturally the Professor had not related them in the terms I have used to explain them. Besides, the guests would have been in no position to understand. His report had been entirely similar to the many he had delivered in the course of his career. Everything had been expressed in twisted and ambiguous terms. Once again what had emerged was a complex and baroque liturgy, intended only to lead up to the final announcement.

As always happened in his most solemn moments, the Professor could not resist the temptation to clothe even his more sincere remarks in courtly words: "This is the state of the Party as of a week ago. It is certainly not brilliant, but neither is it catastrophic, when you consider that we have been in power for more than thirty years. And if the Party appears bruised and battered, it still maintains a secret strength of its own. And if we have lost many adherents and many followers, as unfortunately happens to those no longer able to keep their promises, it is also true that we are still ruling the government, with the consent of all other parties. The less we are loved the more we prove to be indispensable. We have every right to boast that we have never had recourse to force in order to stay in power. This is the Party I leave you, and forgive me if it is not the Party I would have liked to leave you.

"It is not without profound regret," concluded the Professor, stressing his words, "that I announce to you my irrevocable decision to relinquish the helm of the Party, which you have insistently entrusted to me so many times, to retire into meditation and prayer in the monastery of La Verna.* I have indeed ended by accepting the fond invitation of the father prior, who has urged me to fresco the walls and vaults of a chapel. It is not without deep emotion that I take leave of you, my beloved friends, after having dedicated the best years of my life to the good of the Party and the country. Perhaps with fluctuating success, but always with the same will and tenacity."

In uttering these last words, the Professor had spread out both his arms, in a gesture that was already sacerdotal. And at this point all the guests understood that they would have to kiss him.

* Famous monastery, built on a site given to Saint Francis in 1213, in the province of Arezzo. (Tr.)

"**O**h no you don't!" This exclamation resounded in the room just as the Professor was implanting a kiss on the cheek of the minister of justice. The Professor jerked back, turning toward the door on the right, where someone had entered. I must say it was the first time in years that I had seen him jump.

His astonishment, however, was justified. From the door on the right came Berlinguer, Amendola, Pajetta, Ingrao, Natta, Cossutta—in short, the whole group that the Professor and I had encountered at the meeting in Via delle Botteghe Oscure. Antonino Tatò, who remained on guard in the corridor, made me a timid sign of greeting before closing the door.

We had hardly recovered from that surprise when the Professor was again obliged to jump, on hearing a second exclamation, this one coming from the left and uttered with a strong German accent even we could detect: "No way!" From that door entered five individuals all in black overcoats, all with hats pulled down over their eyes and with their faces muffled in gray scarves. Four of them stationed themselves along the sides, their backs to the wall, their hands in their pockets, their legs wide apart. The fifth took a few steps forward, removing his hat and pulling off his scarf. Henry Kissinger was back in our midst.

The Professor no longer knew where to look. The deep flush that had spread over his face, quite visible despite his white beard, showed he was in a state of great confusion and extreme embarrassment. With a vague and altogether unconvincing gesture, he made a sign to the unexpected guests to be seated around the table, but no one took him up on it. The Communists merely took another step forward; Kissinger did the same from the opposite side.

"Oh no you don't," repeated Berlinguer. "No way!" echoed Kissinger.

From being red-faced, the Professor went pale. Dropping into his chair, he prepared to listen to the charges Berlinguer was about to bring against him.

"If I'm not mistaken," Berlinguer began, "it was you, and you alone, who explained surrender plan number three to those standing before you. True or false?" The disheartened Professor nodded his head. "If I'm not mistaken, it was you, and you alone, who asked that our two parties come to an agreement to postpone the elections and guarantee the stability of the Center-Left framework. And it was you who assured me and my comrades that this pact would be respected. True or false?" But the Professor had no wish to deny it, even if he would have preferred not to listen.

While Berlinguer was speaking, one of the Americans along the wall had approached Kissinger and whispered something in his ear. Obviously he was translating what Berlinguer had said so far. The Communist party secretary courteously paused, waiting for the other to finish whispering.

When he began again, Berlinger had still harsher things to say.

"My dear Professor, *pacta sunt servanda*. And our pact provided that any eventual variation in the political framework could not be decided without our consent. It was you yourself who said that power would be left lying on the floor and that we could pick it up whenever we liked. Such words don't lend themselves to equivocation: we, and only we, would be the ones to decide the moment to announce those elections that, in your own judgment, would bring us to power. True or false?"

This time Berlinguer went on without even waiting for a sign of assent. "Let it be clear, absolutely clear," he intoned, "that we have no intention of going back on the agreement you signed, and we have no intention of letting you, its principal and perhaps only guarantor, go off and fresco the monastery of La Verna. We're sorry, but your place is elsewhere.

"Instead it's our firm intention to make this political framework still more stable and lasting, while you, with your absurd proposal to retire, would certainly have helped to destroy it. On the contrary, we intend to strengthen your power still more, in the higher interests of the nation.

"It is our will that within a month, no more, you yourself, Professor, put your shoulder to an operation that we have already examined and prepared down to the last detail, an operation that will put an end to the grave crisis that has struck our country and will signal the beginning of recovery. We have had it drawn up and ready for a long time. Now it is up to you to carry it out."

The silence of a tomb descended on the room. Bertolon and the ministers sat erect in their chairs, their arms on the table, motionless as so many stone guests. The Professor made an effort to regain his calm, to return to being the gruff, intractable man I had known in his most difficult moments. Kissinger stood slightly bent so as not to lose a single word of the translation being whispered in his ear.

"Today," Berlinguer resumed implacably, "I will explain to you only the strategic lines of this operation. The working details will be communicated to you in due course. But let it be clear from now on that next month, on a date still to be set, you, Professor, will appear on television at eight-thirty p.m., after the announcer informs the audience that the program is being interrupted for an urgent communication. You, Professor, will read to the Italians the following communiqué: 'A few hours ago, the prime minister and the minister of the interior announced that a plot to carry out a coup d'état has been uncovered. Thanks to the promptness and vigilance of our government and to the decisive intervention of our glorious armed forces, I can inform you with legitimate pride that this vile attack on our democratic institutions has been successfully foiled. As I speak to you, thousands of conspirators are being rounded up. Fighting is in progress to overcome the last hotbeds of resistance. To guarantee the safety of the population, the ministers of defense and of the interior, with the prime minister's consent, have ordered four days of curfew. The defense of public order has been entrusted to our glorious armed forces alone. *Carabinieri* and police will remain confined to their barracks. The armed forces have received the order to shoot on sight anyone who dares to break the curfew. In the face of this infamous attack on our institutions, the president and prime minister have asked me to assume full powers. In the higher interests of the nation, I have thought it my duty to accept. And I order that from this moment all constitutional guarantees be suspended indefinitely, until such time as public order, the indispensable safeguard of prosperity and social progress, can be re-established.' "

Berlinguer came forward again, to hand the Professor the sheet of paper with the text of the communiqué. Without turning a hair, the Professor folded it carefully and put it in his wallet. Kissinger, who so far had been paying the strictest attention to the translation, raised his head. The lenses of his glasses had a sinister glitter.

"**M**y dear Professor," Berlinguer went on in a calmer voice, "you can rest assured that your television appearance will take place without any danger to your person. As you go before the microphones, five thousand paratroopers, commanded by a general loyal to us, will have taken up positions surrounding Via Teulada.* Your safety in the studios will be guaranteed by the usual efficiency and discretion of my party's security forces. If you carry out the instructions you've just received and those you'll receive later, loyally and with discipline, you can be certain from now on that everything will turn out for the best, both for you and for your friends."

In uttering these words, Berlinguer even tried to venture a smile. The results of this effort seemed to me debatable, but in any case they were enough to reanimate the stone guests a little. Some of them even dared to light cigarettes.

"My dear Professor," Berlinguer went on in a more relaxed tone, "we've now told you what you must do. As far as we're concerned, with full respect for that pact we freely signed, the matter could even be considered closed. But we mean to satisfy your curiosity, which besides is legitimate. Having explained to you what you'll have to do, we'll tell you why you have to do it.

"You're dying to know why I won't be the one to appear on television next month to announce this suspension of con-

* Location of the RAI-TV studios in Rome. (Tr.)

stitutional rights, which will certainly be very long and, God forbid, may even be final. Well, I can answer that immediately.

"We know, we've always known, that hard times were in store for our unhappy country and that only through much suffering would the Italian workers be able to recover their lost industriousness and at least part of their lost prosperity. You can hardly expect us, with our past and our seriousness, to approve in the slightest this state of permanent anarchy into which Italy has been thrown by your foolishness and the demagoguery of others. But we would offend you by saying that you yourself have had such a cheap and superficial concept of our programs and intentions. You've always known that one fine day we would say *enough*, and that then we'd act. What you never imagined is that we would say *enough* and not act openly, but through a third party.

"You see, Professor, any truly revolutionary uprising, any effective overthrow of a system, requires a brutal and painful rending of the social fabric. The suspension of civil rights, the elimination of dissent, the suppression of trade-union autonomy, the disciplining of the press, the reinforcement of the police, the establishment of labor camps for those who have been drugged by anarchy and lost all will and capacity for work are not tragic errors, as even we now have to say in our election rallies. Unfortunately, they are unavoidable decisions, whenever certain circumstances occur, whenever a regime doesn't hold together and it has not yet been possible to build a new one. Stalin, whom we no longer honor but whom we have never forgotten, was by no means the monster your propaganda has tried to paint. Comrade Stalin was merely a surgeon of history.

"And today when this regime is collapsing, it is up to

you, at least officially, to assume the task of building another. We have decided on this because we're the first to realize that, given the particular situation of our country, certain operations can be conducted only behind a façade, so as to avoid international complications that inevitably would get out of everyone's control. You can see besides that this impromptu meeting is being attended, surely accidentally, by an authoritative representative of the American government, and I'm sure that he, on this point at least, will be in perfect agreement."

Everyone turned to Kissinger, who nodded his head.

"But I would be lying," Berlinguer went on, "were I to say that this is the only reason why we intend to keep governing through a third party. There's another reason, a more private, more intimate one, which perhaps I'm wrong to tell you, but I'll tell you all the same. Both I and these comrades of mine have already experienced, as Party members, the harsh years in which the foundations of so many socialist societies were laid, at a cost of much blood and tears. We have seen many other surgeons of history besides Stalin at work.

"Now we prefer that others take up the scalpel and probe the sores. Furthermore, we believe that it's only right. You were the ones to soil Italy; you should be the ones to clean it up with your own hands. We will confine ourselves to presenting you with the programs you'll have to carry out, writing the speeches you're going to have to make, and eventually submitting to you the lists of enemies that you will have to round up.

"Professor, to you will go the high honor of founding the Second Italian Republic, which will be much more efficient than the first, but perhaps a little different from the one you must surely have dreamed of at some moments in your political career. You will not be loved, since crowds love only merciful doctors, but we will protect you, and if need be, defend you. But, under our guidance, you will also be able to manifest your well-known dynamism and efficiency to the full. Naturally, the day will come when your wish to return to painting will be granted. But you will allow us to decide that ourselves."

Having finished his speech, Berlinguer turned his back on the Professor and the guests and headed rapidly for the door before anyone had a chance to answer him. But standing on the threshold, Berlinguer turned back and added: "By this time, some one of you could have raised an objection: We don't go along with you, we're not available, you'll have to be the ones to dirty your hands. But, as you see, we didn't even take that possibility into consideration. You're too fatuous to tear yourselves away from your posts. You're too cynical not to be available for anything. And too cowardly to face our anger."

Part Three

I write these pages, these last pages, in room 713 in the Palmiro Togliatti Residence, where, along with myself, many other faithful servants of the state find hospitality. Since the day I had the honor of attending the inauguration of the Rome-Palestrina subway, I have left my post of first private secretary at the ministry of planning and am now enjoying a deserved rest. I am more than seventy years old, and a few weeks ago I celebrated, together with my new friends in the residence, the advent of the year 2000.

This chronicle of mine will find an indifferent reception among the younger generation, although it contains many details that are unknown to most people and that, in any case, no one before me has told. But the vicissitudes of the First Republic, often so complicated, do not interest young people at all, partly because they have had the good fortune to live in a much simpler and cleaner society, partly because at school they have surely been unable to understand, much less love, the recent past of their country.

Their teachers speak of it with detachment, without making an effort to go deeper or interpret. The boys and girls have to stay up all night memorizing the names of the forty-three prime ministers who alternated in power from 1945 to 1980, and they do not succeed in understanding the reason for all these frantic rotations. And those Dorotei, Morotei, Piccolinians, Tavianians, Fanfanians, Basicists, New Forcists, and such, who pullulate in the textbooks or crowd the footnotes at the bottom of the page, understandably exasperate them.

Once they have passed their examinations, the young people do not want to hear any more about them.

Educators are divided: there are those who maintain that the study of the First Republic and of its current geography (how the Professor loved that adjective!) constitutes an excellent mental exercise; others reply that then it would be better to train young minds by bringing back the logarithm tables. It is probable that the second thesis will prevail and that in future textbooks the thirty-five years of the First Republic will be summarized in a few pages. Which means that of those many prime ministers whom I knew so well, not even the names would remain.

Even men of my generation, though they lived along with me through those experiences, do not feel any nostalgia for them. If there is anything they like to recall from those now remote years, it is the championship soccer games. Even among my new friends in the Palmiro Togliatti Residence, these pages of mine will find only a few, inattentive readers.

Nor do I expect that my notes will be received with any interest by politicians and the historians themselves. Any mention of this work at one of the many academic congresses is quite out of the question. If then I had decided to write and publish this book while I was still working in the public administration, I would have committed a grave error. No one would have reprimanded me, but my career would most certainly have suffered.

The position taken by politicians and historians with regard to the Professor is indeed a special one. They all recognize the great merits of the founder of the Second Republic, who in seven years of hard work succeeded in avoiding the collapse of Italy and in creating the conditions for the Great Leap Forward, and as a result for the Great Restructuring.

The monastery of La Verna, where the Professor serenely passed the last years of his life, has become a national monument, and groups of young Party activists are taken there every Sunday to admire the frescoes he painted in the naves and on the ceiling of a chapel. *Workers of the World Unite, in the Name of the Lord,* the great composition that covers the entire ceiling and recalls, however vaguely, Michelangelo's frescoes in the Sistine Chapel, arouses respectful admiration. Art-history textbooks speak of it at great length.

The block of marble that the Professor had wrapped up in Piazza del Gesù has been set up in the Piazza dei Bottoni,* so called because surrounded by that complex of skyscrapers housing the twelve thousand functionaries of the Ministry of Planning, and precisely where the famous room of the buttons is to be found. In this piazza, which has become the pulsing heart of our national life, the huge monolith, marked by so many vigorous blows of the chisel, arouses great interest and curiosity.

Scholars are divided. Some maintain that what we have here is a work barely sketched out, a work which the Professor was obliged to leave uncompleted, having been called to the much more important task of forging, in the flesh, the image of a new Italy. Thus, according to these scholars, the work could be said to have great historical value, but no artistic value. Others, however, assert that though it is true the Professor had been called to much higher assignments, he was well aware of leaving in Piazza del Gesù a block of marble to which posterity would inevitably end by linking his name. If the Professor had not had it destroyed, and indeed had personally seen to wrapping it, there must have been a reason for it, and it was cer-

* "Buttons Square." (Tr.)

tainly a reason of an aesthetic kind. Besides, for those who knew how to look, the monolith expressed a repressed and yet bursting strength, so as indeed to become the most symbolic and enduring artistic testimony of that period when men tried but did not succeed in molding the social reality of the country.

Supporters of the historical thesis insist that the Professor, on that January afternoon in 1980, wrapped the monolith in a plastic sheet simply to keep the dust off it. Those who uphold the aesthetic thesis maintain that, on the contrary, the sheet of plastic too has a precise significance, being the dismal sudarium deposited over a great but failed ambition. The result is that tourists who rush to the Piazza dei Bottoni to admire the monolith sometimes see it naked and sometimes wrapped. It all depends on which school of thought prevails at that moment in the New Academy.

These discussions, so rich and stimulating, of the Professor as artist are not equally matched by debates on the Professor as statesman. Scholars who concern themselves with him always speak at length about the early years of his political life, and in particular they have praised his association with Dossetti and La Pira,* whom, as everyone knows, Pope John XXV has recently beatified. On the other hand, what his biographers call "the years of unrealized accomplishments," from about 1960 to 1980, have still not been studied with the necessary care. His work as the founder of the Second Republic has certainly been given its proper importance, but I would not say it has yet been placed in a precise historical perspective. We skip a little too quickly over the operation that brought about constitutional reform, and especially over

---

* La Pira, former mayor of Florence, and Dossetti, a catholic theorist, were members of the left wing of the Christian Democrat party. (Tr.)

the sometimes rough methods that became necessary for building the foundations of the new order. Our historical studies are entirely clear and exhaustive only when they begin to speak of the man who succeeded the.Professor, the man who inspired the Great Leap Forward: Enrico Berlinguer.

In short, this chronicle of mine will neither find favor with the public nor be of interest to scholars: perhaps it will not even find a publisher disposed to print it. But I go on just the same. The need to clarify the meaning of those events, of which for so many years I was the witness and participant, is by now irresistible, if only to myself. Even if, except for myself, no one seems to be interested.

All went according to the script. Nineteen days after the meeting at the Farnesina, the Professor read on television that little sheet of paper that he had kept in his wallet. There was no lack of dramatic moments: severe clashes took place between security forces of the Communist party and battalions of police and *carabinieri* supported by groups of radical students and some divisions of metal workers. The most heated battles occurred at Mirafiori in Turin and in the steelworks of Sampierdarena. No one ever knew the number of the fallen, which was surely high. But it would be an exaggeration to speak of civil war. In the industrial belt around Milan there were ambushes and killings that went on for at least two years, but the new police forces, completely reorganized, were able to put an end to these incidents of urban guerrilla warfare. No one ever bothered the American soldiers stationed in Verona, Naples, and all the other bases of the Atlantic Alliance.

Neither the Soviet nor the American government interfered in the slightest in our domestic affairs; the United States, indeed, continued to distribute its usual loans, while asking as guarantee the last works of art still available in our museums. Economic relations between the United States and Italy were resolved with mutual satisfaction at the beginning of the Great Leap Forward, that is to say in the Berlinguer era. By then Italy had no need of the loans. Kissinger, who in the meantime had become president of the United States, had no difficulty in liquidating all the mortgages on our museums, receiving in exchange fifteen paintings by the Professor and two hundred works by Renato Guttuso.*

Throughout the early 1980s, the Professor had every opportunity to give full expression to his energy and dynamism. Constitutional, judicial, scholastic, health, bureaucratic, and fiscal reforms were carried out in record time. It was more difficult to restructure the trade unions, police, and *carabinieri;* a strong hand was necessary on many occasions. It became indispensable to set up labor camps, and many Italians thought to be incorrigible were sent to populate them. According to popular rumor, these camps, officially known as "workers' requalification centers," housed a good two million Italians; but frankly this figure seems to me much too high. But no one has known the exact number, and all my inquiries have turned out to be in vain.

Political restructuring, on the other hand, occurred slowly but in an orderly way, without causing any traumas for the Italians. Two years after the famous communiqué of February 1980, the Professor again appeared on television, to announce that the Christian Democrat party was changing its name and would henceforth be known as the Italian Popular Workers' Party. Membership was open to adherents of all parties in the constitutional spectrum. A special commission would examine all requests to join, and its judgment would be final.

Almost all requests from Communists were accepted; on the other hand, those presented by Socialists, Social Democrats, Republicans, and Liberals were rigorously sifted. President of the Party was the Professor, and Deputy Berlinguer

* Prolific Communist painter known for his realistic scenes of peasant and working-class life. (Tr.)

was named secretary. In an historic appearance in Piazza del Popolo, the Professor and Berlinguer announced to an immense crowd that the Fascist peril was now forever averted. For the occasion, a generous amnesty was granted. Next day the Professor and Berlinguer were received in special audience by John XXV.

The meeting at the foreign-ministry building, amply reported in this chronicle, was thus the matrix of important events. And yet people have always had very little to say about this meeting, and with the passage of time it is no longer mentioned at all. Many details, at first cited confusedly, and later wrapped in a fog of oblivion, have ended by being almost incomprehensible. I will say more. Despite the fact that my memory is still excellent, and despite all the efforts I have made, first on my own, then with the help of my loyal friend Tatò, there are certain details that are not even clear to me.

I can state, without fear of denial, that on that fateful January 20, 1980, the Berlinguer group arrived in great secrecy at the foreign ministry, one hour before the almost simultaneous arrival of Kissinger and the Professor. A few trusted comrades had let them in by a service door on the side and had made them comfortable in a room adjoining the one where the dinner and subsequent meeting took place. My friend Tatò has acknowledged to me that some of these comrades were specialists in electronic techniques, and this enabled the Berlinguer group to listen to and record everything that was said in the room. On the other hand, I have not been able to find out who had informed Berlinguer that the Professor would keep some of the diners at the table after Kissinger's departure. Much less ascertain how Berlinguer knew, or at least suspected, that that evening the Professor would announce his retirement from politics.

Now we come to President Kissinger.* In this case too I have reconstructed all his moves with certainty, and I can tell you how it was that the then secretary of state, who everyone thought was in the helicopter, could make his appearance in the room simultaneously with Berlinguer. As the reader will remember, President Leone, in accordance with the ceremony worked out between the diplomats and trade unionists, had gone up to Kissinger and exclaimed in a loud voice: "I'll come with you. Anyway, we're going the same way." But it will not have escaped the more attentive reader that Leone had said good-bye to Kissinger at the entrance to the stadium, without accompanying him onto the playing field, since this had been demanded by the representatives of the CISL.

Kissinger had seized the opportunity. Realizing that no Italians, not even the attendants, were present on the field as the helicopters were preparing to lift off, the secretary of state had quickly got out and gained the exit, along with four CIA agents. While the stadium attendants were watching the helicopters hovering in the sky (and some brandished their fists and shouted curses), Kissinger and his escort, under cover of darkness, had gone back to the Farnesina. A few old diplomats were there to welcome them and lead them to the other door of the room.

But once again: who had informed Kissinger that such a meeting would take place immediately after his departure? Who had let him know that this meeting would be so important as to require his presence and tacit endorsement? Who had

* The author would seem to suggest that in the 1980s the Americans amended their Constitution to allow a naturalized citizen to ascend to the highest office. (Tr.)

persuaded him to run such undoubtedly serious risks in hostile territory?

I, though I was the custodian of so many secrets, can swear on the Gospels that I knew nothing of it. My friend Tatò, whom I have questioned with fond insistence, swears the same oath on his honor. The Professor always rejected with scorn any suggestion that he was aware of what the Communist and the American had plotted behind his back. Someone has surely lied. But who?

The notion that the Professor, in my absence, had revealed to Bertolon or any minister his intention to announce his retirement from political life is absolutely out of the question. The monks of La Verna knew about it, and one certainly cannot exclude a priori that some agent of the CIA or informer of the Communist party may have been hidden among them.

But to tell the truth, I have mentioned this last hypothesis only out of my scruples as a chronicler. In my opinion, the Professor had known all along that, at the last moment, Kissinger would turn up on one side and Berlinguer on the other to compel him to stay on.